Donland's Victory

By

Perry Comer

ISBN: 9781705576274

In Memory

of

Irby Eugene Comer

(my Dad)

BOOKS BY PERRY COMER

The Prize

The Messenger
Donland and the Hornet

Donland's Ransom
Donland and the Hornet

Raid on Port Royal
Donland and the Hornet

The Bond of Duty
Donland and the Hornet

Siege
Donland and The Hornet

The Rescue
Donland and the Hornet

Donland's Courage

Fall of Fort Fisher
(Juvenile action/adventure)
(Civil War)

Andrew's War
(Juvenile action/adventure)
(Civil War)

Fighting Marines: Hardy's Commission

Fighting Marines: Hardy's Challenge

Chapter One

Donland was accustomed to waiting; today was no exception. He sat and sipped wine while reading an old copy of the *Gazette*. Half of the paper lay on the white tablecloth. The half containing the list of promotions he held in his hand. To his knowledge, his name had never appeared in the publication. It mattered not; he told himself, but inwardly there was a twinge of desire for recognition. His body bore the scars of fights and battles that signified he had on more than one occasion come close to losing limbs or life.

He lifted the glass and drank sadly remembering how he had bargained with the half-pay lieutenant in need of money. The young man was reluctant to part with his uniforms and hats and said, "Were it not for my hunger I'd not part with them. I sacrificed so much for so many years to gain my station and all for naught. They cast me on the beach with a mere half-pay that I'll not receive for another three months." At least, he wasn't as that young man.

Donland regretted the bargain but he was in desperate need having lost all when *Brune's* magazine exploded. Fate was kind to him otherwise he would be as the young lieutenant. The task to act as guide and the subsequent rescue of Lord Ångermanland, the Swedish noble and nephew of England's queen, had brought an unimaginable promise of reward. He was to be made a captain, Admiral Pigot had no choice in the matter and neither would those in the Admiralty. A command was promised and he was to receive new orders this very day.

"Ah, there you are, I thought I would find you here and not in a common man's pub. Still waiting I see!" Jackson said as he pulled a chair from the table and sat.

"Aye, I'd thought you would have appeared before now. Will you have a glass of wine?" Donland asked.

"A tot of rum will do me, that is unless you'd rather I have wine. There be those that watch and I'd not want to lower you in their eyes."

Donland took the bait, "Your insolence is intolerable. Were you under my orders you'd find yourself facing the gratings!"

"Aye, but I'm no longer yours to command, I'm a free and prosperous merchant sailing under the flag of a free nation. Formerly your enemy."

"That may be but the provost would not take kindly to rabble such as you insulting one of the King's officers. Antigua is still under his rule."

A young midshipman entered the inn and made eye contact with Donland. He made straight for him. "Beg pardon, sir, Captain Hood requests your presence aboard *Warrior.*"

Jackson grinned, "Aye, it's about time. My best to you Isaac."

"I'll come," Donland answered the boy and picked up his hat from the table. He felt awkward in another man's freshly laundered, starched and ironed clothes.

The jolly boat was crewed by four men in matching rigs. Each was freshly shaven with their hair pulled back into queuesbeneath tarred hats.

"Give way all!" the midshipman commanded once Donland was seated.

Again he felt ill at ease; these men were strangers to him as was the midshipman. The slight, however, of a midshipman bearing the request to have an audience with Captain Hood instead of lieutenant was not lost on him. It would be this way until he had proven himself worthy of the promotion. Jealousy would be the coin of the day and he must learn to steel himself against the insults.

The boat drifted alongside *Warrior's* massive hull and did not bang. One of the crew grasped the lines and held the boat fast. The midshipman made to rise. Donland placed a hand on the boy's shoulder. The boy turned and the look in his eyes was first one of anger and then of embarrassment as he remembered that he was junior to a lieutenant. One that he knew was not highly favored among his betters. He allowed Donland to rise and take the ladder first.

Warrior's deck was orderly and busy as hands holystoned the deck, coiled cordage and were about other daily tasks. No officer greeted Donland after he saluted the helm and doffed his hat.

"This way," The midshipman said as he stepped in front of Donland and headed for a hatch. It was in Donland's mind to take the youngster to task for the lack of respect but he chose just to get on with the audience with Captain Hood. He dutifully followed the midshipman to the hatch and down. It seemed no one paid any attention to their arrival. The ordinary seaman dutifully knuckled their foreheads as they passed en route to whatever task they were to perform.

The two marine guards at Captain Hood's door snapped to attention either for the midshipman or for Donland. He did not know which and it mattered not. The midshipman knocked.

"Enter," a burly voice called from beyond the door.

The marine on the right of the door reached and opened the door and closed it behind Donland.

"Beg pardon Captain Hood, I have retrieved Lieutenant Donland as you requested," the midshipman stated.

Hood was sitting at his large deck that was mostly covered with logs and papers. Behind him stood Lieutenant Watley, the flag lieutenant.

"That will be all Mister Styles," Watley said to dismiss the midshipman.

Donland stood with his hat in the crook of his arm. Hood was busy reading. Donland was well aquatinted with the practice of keeping a junior officer waiting. Captain Okes, before his death, often kept his lieutenants waiting for as much as a quarter hour.

As Donland waited his eyes took in the fine Persian carpet covering most of the deck and the very expensive mahogany sideboards, upholstered chairs and a cabinet with a glass front containing silver serving pieces and crystal goblets. Captain Hood liked

3

the finer things and could afford them.

Watley's face showed nothing as he remained standing to Captain Hood's right.

Hood, after some five minutes, laid aside the document he was reading. "See to this Mister Watley, it's a trivial matter but one that needs immediate attention."

He leaned back in his chair and studied Donland then pursed his lips. "I've no choice and had I, you would be on the beach no matter the heroics. But, as I have no choice and those above me have no choice you will be granted a captaincy and a command. This is, and you know it to be true, most irregular but I've no say in the matter. Admiral Pigot tasked me with this as he cared not to have his name associated with the deed. Therefore, I am the one to make your assignment," Hood stated and his face seemed to grow redder with each word.

"Mister Watley, have you the packet?"

"Aye, Captain," Watley answered and picked up a large packet from the corner of Hood's desk.

Hood took the packet from Watley and handed it across to Donland. "I've nothing to add, your orders are contained in the packet. Do your duty, that is all!"

Donland said nothing. He received the packet, saluted and turned for the door.

"Accompany him Mister Watley!" Hood barked.

"Aye, Captain," Watley answered.

"Captain Donland," Watley called just as Donland put his foot on the first rung of the hatchway ladder.

Donland stopped.

"Allow me to congratulate you Sir, on your promotion," Watley said as he extended his hand. "From your record and the exploits I've heard, you are more than deserving. Even if others do not appreciate your service please know that I do," Watley said.

Donland managed a smile and replied, "Decent of you Mister Watley and thank you."

He then followed Donland to the deck and saw him over the side.

Sitting in the stern of the jolly boat, Donland tucked the packet inside his coat. He decided to wait and examine the contents when he was ashore. Perhaps, if Jackson were still at the inn, he would relate the events aboard *Warrior* but he would not share anything about the audience with Hood to no other.

Jackson was still sitting at the table in the Queen Anne's dining room. He smiled upon seeing his friend and asked, "Do you have it? What ship?"

Rather than answer, Donland sat.

The serving maid came to the table and Donland said, "Brandy if you please and bring the bottle."

"From that I would judge it did not go well," Jackson stated.

Donland removed his hat and stretched out his legs. "Not as I expected," he said.

"You've not answered, have you a ship?"

Donland pulled the packet from his coat. "Your knife if you please."

Surprised, Jackson obeyed and produced his knife and held it out to Donland handle first.

Taking the knife, Donland carefully lifted the wax seal and opened the packet. There were several documents, he examined the first one. It was a temporary captain's commission effective upon receipt until such a time as confirmed or denied by the admiralty. He laid it aside and examined the second document. He was ordered to take command of *Oxford* a fourth rate of fifty-four guns now in Jamaica being refitted.

He said to Jackson, "*Oxford*, a fifty-four, at anchor in Jamaica. Know her?"

"Aye, a hulk more or less!"

Donland nodded and said, "I thought as much."

"They're trying to force you onto the beach," Jackson stated with a hint of anger.

Donland surprised Jackson by smiling. "Aye, they are. Have you seen her?"

"Surely you aren't going to accept?"

"Perhaps, but have you seen her?"

"Aye, I've seen her, she sits at Port Royal over next to the careening wharves. At least that is where she was back two months ago. I don't know anything more."

"It's a start, I'm to take a packet in two days time and join her. That will allow me time to have new uniforms made, two epaulets to

5

be sure."

"Aye, you've more than earned them," Jackson said and grinned.

"What of you?" Donland asked.

"Off with the tide, I've a living to earn," Jackson answered and stood.

Donland also stood and put forth his hand. "Thank you for waiting to share the moment with me, there's only one other that I would be here."

"That I know, she'll be proud nonetheless when the news reaches her."

Jackson shook Donland's hand and turned for the door.

Donland watched as Jackson's back disappeared through the door. He took his seat, lifted his glass and drank. He did not see David until the boy plopped down in the seat vacated by Jackson.

"I could do with a glass," David said.

Donland poured and as he did David asked, "Have you news?"

"Aye," Donland answered. "We are off to Jamaica in two days time. We've time for a visit to the tailor for we both need new uniforms." Donland teased.

David's face lit up with a broad smile, "So, we've a ship?"

"Aye, and I've my step but it will have to be confirmed in London before it's posted. Still, I've little doubt it will be."

"Gawd!" David said while beaming. He added, "Then I'll have a chance to sit for my exam!"

Donland smiled and tempered the boy's dreams, "In time, in time. We've a ship to set to rights first. A fifty-four!"

David's eyes were as wide as saucers, "A fifty-four!"

"Old but she'll do us, will she not?"

"Aye, and more!" David exclaimed with excitement and joy.

"A toast?" Donland asked.

David took the glass and lifted it, "To Captain Donland," he said.

Donland did not reply but drank from his glass.

They were interrupted by a voice from behind, "A celebration?"

Donland turned to see his friend Powell, dressed in a tattered lieutenant's rig. "I thought you've sailed?" Donland asked as he stood.

"For a while," Powell answered as he made his way to a chair. "Seems the new Captain was not pleased with my assessment of his abilities."

Donland sat and motioned for Powell to do likewise. He asked,

"You are unemployed then?"

"Aye, but half-pay," Powell answered and motioned for the serving maid to bring another glass.

"Did you not resign your commission?" David asked.

Powell grinned and answered, "No, I considered doing so but was persuaded by Jackson to wait and meet my new captain. I took his advice, so half-pay is better than no pay. To make matters worse, the cards have been unkind."

Donland clapped Powell on the shoulder. "To my good fortune that you've little coin!" David looked on in stunned silence.

The serving girl brought Powell's glass and set it on the table.

"Another bottle of brandy if you please," Donland told the girl and placed a coin in her palm.

She glanced at the coin and smiled then turned away.

"You've something to celebrate?" Powell inquired while filling his glass.

"Aye, and a proposition to put to you since you are not employed," Donland said.

"The cause of celebration?" Powell asked and downed the brandy in a gulp.

"Admiral Pigot has given me a command and I'm to sail for Jamaica in two days by packet to take it up."

Powell's face showed his surprise. "Aye, that is cause to celebrate, another sloop?"

Donland was beaming as he said, "A fifty-four!"

"No!" Powell exclaimed.

"Aye, the *Oxford*, know her?"

"Captain Shaw commanded her until a few months ago," Powell related and continued. "He died of fever as I understand as did a number of his crew. What's your proposition?"

Donland did not miss Powell's keen interest. He answered, "*Oxford* is to be fitted out, I do not know her current state. Perhaps she's already had her bottom scrapped, repaired and is ready for refitting. I'll know after I arrive. Nor do I know her current muster needs but I assume there is room for a lieutenant. As you are unemployed, I recommend you journey with us. Of course, I will pay your passage."

The shock and surprise of the offer was evident on Powell's face. He stammered, "I'd be a fool to refuse."

The girl brought the bottle of brandy and set it on the table. She smiled at David and turned away.

Powell and Donland watched her go. David continued to look after her.

"She fancies you," Powell said.

David's face turned crimson.

Donland studied the boy for a moment, it was the first time he noticed the beginning of a beard. He lifted his glass and drained the contents. David did likewise.

"Let me do the honor," Powell said as he reached for the bottle. He pulled the cork and poured brandy into Donland's glass and then his own.

David looked from Powell to Donland and said, "Sir!"

Donland said with seriousness, "Old enough to fight a man's fight, old enough to drink a man's drink."

"Aye," Powell agreed and poured brandy into David's glass.

"Then it's settled, you will accompany us?" Donland asked Powell.

"Aye, and with great pleasure Captain," Powell said and suddenly looked surprised. "Captain!" He blurted, "You've your step!"

"Aye," Donland stated and lifted his glass. "To *Oxford!*"

"Aye," Powell and David answered in unison.

Chapter Two

"Morant Bay, just there!" Powell said and pointed.

"We are close then?" Donland asked.

Powell turned to him, "Aye but we'll not see *Oxford* until we've tacked and entered the roads."

Donland contained his excitement but David and Simon did not, the young men climbed into the shrouds for a better view. David had borrowed a glass.

The previous evening over supper, Johnson, the packet owner and captain, stated that *Oxford* had received no attention in the time that she sat anchored at Port Royal. When Donland pressed for more information, Johnson said that he did not know if she was in fact seaworthy but did know an anchor watch was maintained. "You'll be needing a whole crew," he remarked as he rose to offer after-dinner cigars.

Donland declined the cigar and said, "I've a first officer, a midshipman and a coxs'un. A good start by my reckoning."

After supper, he spoke with Powell about serving as *Oxford's* first. His hope was that Powell would be senior to whatever officers remained of *Oxford's* former company. Should that obstacle be overcome, there remained the Admiralty's confirmation. Which brought to mind his concern of not being confirmed as captain of *Oxford*. Commodore Pettibone, who commanded the anchorage, wharfs and stores on Port Royal, was under naval regulations governing foreign ports. He could appointment lieutenants to vessels and forward those appointments to the Admiralty. But, he could do nothing to aid Donland in his confirmation. Only time would tell if the

Admiralty agreed with his appointments. In any case, confirmations took months as ships bearing requests crossed the Atlantic and others returned with the Admiralty decisions. There were no guarantees for the Admiralty could send their own choices. Those appointed by someone such as Commodore Pettibone would end up on the beach.

"Will you be going straightway to *Oxford?*" Honest asked.

The question dragged Donland from his thoughts of the previous evening. "No, I'm to deliver a dispatch to Commodore Pettibone before going aboard," Donland answered.

"Know what's in it?" Honest asked.

Donland merely answered, "It's sealed."

"Aye, but seals are made of wax," Honest teased.

"Wax they may be but honor is like iron, you'd not understand."

"Honor I know, better than most," Honest answered. "Else, I'd not be standing on this deck!"

"Prepare to tack starboard!" Johnson shouted to his crew interrupting the conversation.

Honest turned his attention to the land. "We'll likely see her soon," he said.

"Aye," Donland answered without revealing his trepidation as he held down his desire to be excited. There was much he did not know and much he hoped for.

The tack was accomplished and the packet nosed into the swells toward the anchorage. Overhead, fluffy low clouds floated on light breezes and between them were patches of bright blue sky.

"Storms before nightfall," Powell remarked.

"Aye," Honest acknowledged.

Donland did not add to the speculation as his mind was fixed upon the meeting with Pettibone. From previous encounters, he had liked the man and respected him. Their paths had not crossed in several years but he had no doubts about Pettibone remembering him. But, he did not know what was in the packet from Hood or what instructions Hood was sending regarding *Oxford*. The packet troubled him.

"There!" David called and pointed.

Powell, Donland and Honest each gripped the railing and strained to see *Oxford*.

She was as Donland expected, even distant she appeared to be in a sad state. There were no sails on her masts. She appeared to be down in her bow with her stern riding high.

"She's a good amount of water in her," Powell remarked.

Donland did not answer. He studied her as they came nearer. Some of her ports were open. Glass was missing from her stern windows. There were dangling lines in her rigging.

"She'll require mor'n a bit of make and mend," Honest said.

"Aye, all a dockyard can provide," Powell added.

"Honest, see to our dunnage," Donland said choosing again not to add to the speculation.

He then called to David, "Mister Welles come down and prepare to go ashore!"

"Aye!" David answered.

Donland lingered on the deck for a few minutes while the others went below to prepare for going ashore. He recalled Jackson's question as to whether or not he would accept *Oxford*. He felt then that there was really no choice if he were to remain an officer in the king's service. Like the young officer who sold his uniforms, the sacrifices to gain his station were not easily discarded. Hood attempted, by assigning him to *Oxford*, to discard those sacrifices and choose personal honor above them. Hood was wrong.

Donland was under no illusion that *Oxford* was meant to be a source of discouragement. There were half-pay captains on the beach capable of fitting *Oxford* out for sea. If that were Hood's intention but it wasn't. Hood's assignment was meant to punish and humiliate. What remained to be seen was what Hood wrote in his letter to Commodore Pettibone.

Billowing clouds were thickening overhead as Donland stepped from the boat to the quay. He stood for a moment studying the anchorage and the careening wharfs.

"The commodore's office is just down there," Powell stated.

"Aye, let us be about it then," Donland answered and started off with his hand resting on the hilt of the new sword.

"Do you suppose he'll remember us?" Powell asked.

"Aye, he will," Donland replied. He was in fact relying on Pettibone to remember him with fondness. If not, refitting *Oxford* would be near impossible. Everything the old ship would need would have to be approved by Pettibone.

"Nervous?" Donland asked Powell as they approached the building.

"Aye, I'd not want this place to be the end of me. I've seen quite a few blue jackets observing our passing. There's no shortage of lieutenants lounging about. Any one of them would take my place beside you. And I do not doubt that the commodore has made promises to a few."

"Seniority will count for something," Donland said in way of assurance. "*Oxford* will require four lieutenants, perhaps five."

Powell said with humor in his voice, "I'll happily accept the fifth."

The marine sentries snapped to attention upon seeing Donland's two epaulets. It was a new experience for him and he hoped this would not be his last.

"Captain Donland, just arrived from Antigua with dispatches from Admiral Pigot," Donland announced to the clerk sitting at a table in the outer office.

"Commodore Pettibone is expecting you," the clerk said as he rose from the chair. "This way Captain," he said as he stepped to the door then knocked.

"Come!" Pettibone called and the clerk opened the door.

Powell and Donland brushed past the clerk and saluted Pettibone as he rose from his chair.

The office was surprising as it contained several paintings of ships and three ships in bottles. On the floor was an exquisite yellow and red carpet with a blue diamond in the center. The desk was ringed with four leather chairs and overhead was a small crystal chandelier.

"Prize money and cargo," Pettibone said with a broad smile. "I've done well as I see by your epaulets that you have as well. I did not expect you to make the step so soon."

"Aye," Donland answered as he glanced at the right epaulet.

"Sit, shall we drink to your success?" Pettibone said as he moved to a mahogany sideboard containing several crystal glasses and a crystal container filled with a light brown liquid.

"Thank you Sir," Donland said allowing some pent-up tension to drain as he sat.

"Mister Powell, sit and join us," Pettibone said as he began to pour.

Powell sat and gladly accepted the glass; his mouth was dry.

"You've dispatches?" Pettibone said as he handed Donland a glass.

"Aye, Sir," Donland answered and fished in his coat for the envelope.

Pettibone took the packet, examined it and moved behind his desk. "You would that I open it now?" he asked.

The glass was half-way to his lips but he halted and answered. "I wish to God I did not but that sealed packet has kept me awake for two nights."

Pettibone nodded and picked up a small knife. He slipped the blade under the seal and pealed away the oilskin. There were three sheets. The first two he laid aside and read the third.

"You are to have the *Oxford*, but you know that." Pettibone said and pursed his lips before continuing. "Admiral Pigot instructs me to fulfill the requirements of all other vessels before giving any attention to the *Oxford*. You are to read yourself in to the anchor watch and remain aboard until such time as careening is commenced. Once the *Oxford* is seaworthy, I am to fill her compliment, stores and power."

Donland listened and was not surprised as he had expected something similar. Powell looked from Pettibone to Donland but did not speak.

"I would say the admiral has something against you. Perhaps you will enlighten me?" Pettibone said staring into Donland's eyes.

"Aye Sir, I shall do so without bitterness or rancor for I have none. I've my step and that alone will do me for now. But as to Admiral Pigot's instructions, I can say he was placed in a difficult position. Some weeks ago I was ordered to act as guide for Captain Sheffield of the *Brune*. We were to land east of San Juan and rescue a Lord Ångermanland of Sweden and favorite nephew of our queen. *Brune*, Captain Sheffield and most of the crew were lost to enemy fire while we were ashore. I, along with a handful of others extracted the young lord and returned him to Antigua. Once there, Angermanland maneuvered, without my knowledge, Admiral Pigot into promoting me and giving me a worthy command. The admiral had little choice since the young man was the queen's nephew so, he complied and my promotion is yet to be confirmed. Which explains his letter to you and the reason for his instructions."

"A pickle!" Pettibone said with a grin.

"Aye," Donland said and sipped from his glass.

"Then Captain Donland we shall comply with our instructions. You may go across and read yourself in. Presently, Lieutenant Almonds, the provost, supplies the anchor watch. You may speak with him about the men he sends aboard. But first, explain Lieutenant Powell's presence."

Donland downed the remains of the glass. "You are no doubt aware of the Admiralty's decision to shed vessels not built by British hands. *Hornet* and *Stinger* fell into that category so Lieutenant Powell and I found ourselves destined for the beach. He found brief employment with the Americans but decided the captain was a fool. I asked him to come here with me in hopes of having him come aboard *Oxford*. It seems his journey was for naught."

Pettibone nodded and said, "Perhaps not, I shall read through the other dispatches and give thought to *Oxford* and Mister Powell."

"Thank you, Sir," Donland said and rose from the chair. "Before you go," Pettibone said. "Your step was more than earned. The way you received it may trouble some but I am not counted among them. I am delighted to serve with you again and wish you great success."

Powell followed Donland from the office and once outside said, "I believe the commodore is sympathetic to our plight and will seek to aid us."

Donland replied, "Aye, he is a good and decent fellow. He knows our records and us. But, let us not venture too far from what is and what is possible. Commodore Pettibone is bound by the admiral's instructions and he'll not lose his position just to aid us. To do so would spell the end to his career."

"Aye," Powell agreed and asked, "How shall we proceed?"

"As the commodore has instructed, we shall go aboard."

Chapter Three

Powell secured a boat to take them out to *Oxford*. Donland, as customary, sat aft in the boat. Powell sat next to him and David, Honest and Simon sat amidships. Just as the boat was tying onto *Oxford's* chains, the storm broke drenching the four.

Donland ignored the rain as he climbed from the boat onto another that was also tied to the ladder. He swung onto the ladder and climbed up the hull and through the sally port. Powell and David followed him. There was no twitter of pipes or a side party to greet them. The deck was empty of men.

"They'll be in the main cabin!" Powell said.

The rain fell as a deluge soaking every man to the skin. Honest produced a whistle from his pocket and blew a blast.

"No matter," Donland said to Powell and pulled the order from his pocket, he did not bother to take it from the oilskin packet. "Captain Isaac Donland is hereby ordered by Admiral Pigot to assume command of His Majesty's ship *Oxford*!" He read loudly and shoved the oilskin back into his coat.

Still no one ventured from the cabin or from below, Donland doubted they even heard the boat bump alongside or the reading in. "Let us get out of this weather!" He shouted to be heard about the rain and thunder.

Powell followed Donland up the ladder from the waist to the quarterdeck. Before he pushed open the door, he heard laughter inside the main cabin. Even in the dim light Donland saw that the quarterdeck was in disarray and strewn with trash. The smell of rotting food, piss and feces was almost overpowering.

He pushed open the cabin door to discover six men and four women in varying states of undress and intercourse. Bottles of rum were strewn on the floor and several tankards littered the table and sideboards. A piece of sailcloth was nailed across the transom windows to keep the rain out.

Powell pushed past Donland, drew his sword and shouted, "Stand to you blaggards!"

The laughter subsided except for one woman's shrill laugh. The man nearest her pushed her to the floor and stood swaying.

"Sir?" Powell asked Donland.

Donland studied the faces of the men, anger boiled inside. "I'll not have the likes of you aboard again! Take your whores and take to the boat! Either go or Lieutenant Powell will run you through!"

"Suh!" one of the drunkards slurred.

Donland drew his sword and pointed it at the man. "Go!" he said constraining his anger.

The men looked one to another; one tugged his trousers up and began buckling his belt. The one naked woman rolled from a makeshift cot and found a pair of trousers. While sitting she began to pull them on, her heavy breasts swaying with every movement. A thin man looked down at the woman and then at Donland. He made to speak, thought better of it, and hurried from the cabin. The others followed. The woman who pulled on the trousers came last, still bare-chested.

"Honest, see them over the side!" Donland barked.

"Aye, Captain!" Honest answered.

He turned to Powell, "Once the storm subsides, I want you to go across to the provost for more men. He'll not send men to clear away this filth so while you are about the town, secure us a few men for the task. I'll have to pay them from my purse but that is of no consequence. Men only, if you please."

Powell slipped his sword back into the scabbard and asked, "What of our dunnage?"

"We will assist you," Donland answered and slapped Powell on the back. "We've done worse as middies!"

"Aye," Powell answered.

Honest and Donland held lanterns high as they went down into the depths of the ship to inspect the hull and see how much water was in the well. What they discovered came as no surprise. The filth and disarray was disgusting. It was so bad that both men were forced to tie handkerchiefs over their noses and mouths. Rats and mice scurried to and fro as the light reached them.

Water in the bow was nigh on four feet deep and it was close to a foot deep aft.

"They've not pumped her in a month of Sundays!" Honest stated.

"Aye, left her to rot and I'm sure there will be a goodly amount of rot. Once she's laid over, if ever, she may be found not worth the coin to repair," Donland said as he crept forward.

Something white caught his attention and he bent over and held the lantern near the water to get a better look. "Look here," he said and pointed. "A skull!"

Honest peered down, "Aye, been here long enough for the rats to have cleaned the bones. May be more than one down here. We'll not know until we get her pumped. I'd put money on this one being some whore."

Donland was disgusted with the thought but he agreed with Honest's assessment. Men like those they encountered in the main cabin would think nothing of beating some woman to death if she was augmentative or belligerent for not being paid.

"Let us go back to the cabin, I've seen all I care to see," Donland said as he turned to go.

"How will we get her pumped if we have no men?" Honest asked as they reached the first hatchway.

"We'll get men," Donland answered.

"You've not that much money in the banks."

Donland laughed and said, "I've no idea how much and what I do have, I'll not waste on paying men to pump. I believe Commodore Pettibone will find some way to assist us.

"He better and soon before this old girl turns turtle and sinks."

The rain ended while Donland and Honest inspected the holds. They went on deck rather than endure the stench of the main cabin. Lines were strewn about the deck, tackle lay in disarray and broken pottery and glass seemed to be everywhere. There was even moss growing on portions of the deck.

"Gawd what a mess!" Honest exclaimed.

"I'm sure the commodore is not aware of these conditions," Donland said.

"Aye, but that provost should be and should have done something afore now!" Honest said as he surveyed the length of *Oxford's* main deck. "No boats, Sir,"

"Aye, I recorded their absence when I came aboard. But we shall have them back if they've not been sunk. As to the provost he shall be aboard tomorrow as will the commodore."

Honest was aghast, "Not to dine!"

Donland laughed, he laughed so hard tears formed in the corners of his eyes.

"That funny was it?" Honest asked.

Donland sucked in a lung of air and held it. He managed to reply, "They'd swing me up from the yard if I did. No, I'll insist they come aboard to see for themselves the lack of attention *Oxford* has received. I would imagine there will be a new provost by the next noon."

"Aye," Honest agreed.

A boat bumped alongside.

"That will be Lieutenant Powell," Donland said and went to the railing.

Powell sat in the stern of the crowded boat. Two other boats were following in the wake of Powell's boat. David and Simon were in the second boat. All three boats were crammed with men.

Powell came through the sally port first followed by a lieutenant and a midshipman. Donland eyed all three. They came to him and saluted and he returned their salutes.

"Lieutenant Brunson of the *Oxford* and Midshipman Hornsby also of *Oxford*. Lieutenant Brunson was second," Powell introduced the newcomers. Hornsby, by Donland's estimate appeared to be almost as old as Brunson and guessed their ages to be no more than twenty-three.

Behind them came the clatter of men and their dunnage coming aboard.

Powell turned to Donland and explained, "These are what remain of the company, twenty-seven all tolled. Commodore Pettibone met me when I came ashore and had these waiting. He said that they were on the muster book and no one could find fault with him for returning them to duty."

"Aye, I knew he would be of assistance and these are a start," Donland said.

He was thoughtful for a moment and looked out over the anchorage. "Mister Powell, set half of them to putting the gun deck in order. Open all ports, we need airing out. After that I want the main cabin cleaned and mopped! Mister Hornsby and Mister Welles will supervise the gun deck cleaning. Set the other half of the men to putting the quarterdeck, waist and forecastle to rights. We'll not bring the boats aboard until all is accomplished."

"Aye, Captain," Powell answered.

Lieutenant Brunson's face showed no emotion. Donland asked, "Date of your commission?"

Brunson did not hesitate and said in a deep baritone, "Lieutenant Powell is senior by several years."

"Then second you shall remain, you will attend to the work on the quarterdeck and have the watch." Donland said. He then asked, "Why have you not been aboard?"

"I've only recently recovered from fever as have the men who came across with me. We were in quarantine and confined to a house in the jungle. As miserable a place as ever existed, we were even guarded. Mister Hornsby was ashore because of a mishap that resulted in breaking a leg. Commodore Pettibone thought it best that he not come back aboard until it mended."

"Then you know little of what has occurred aboard while you were quarantined?"

"That is so, Captain."

Donland half-smiled and said, "You can tell me more of what occurred and about your quarantine at another time. For now, we have a great deal on our plate to make *Oxford* habitable."

"Aye, Captain, Brunson agreed.

Donland addressed Powell, "It will be dark in a couple of hours. Honest and I have examined the holds and there is nothing aboard fit to eat or drink. Select four men and go into the town to buy fresh fruits, meat and bread for our meals tonight and for the morning," Donland said while pulling his purse from his coat. He then counted out some coins.

"Aye, Captain!" Powell said as he received the coins. He put the coins in his pocket then asked, "Rum for the men?"

"Aye, but only a ration for tonight," Donland answered.

Honest returned to the deck after having gone below with Welles and Hornsby. "They should be rid of most of the stench by nightfall. Have you given thought as to our chores for tomorrow?"

"Aye," Donland said. "But now let us go and examine the pumps. Without them we can't proceed."

The wash pump on the deck appeared to be in working order. Donland tested the crank and found that it had suction. It would lend aid to the larger pumps below deck if they were functional.

Honest asked, "Captain will we be dining aboard?"

"Aye, I've sent Lieutenant Powell ashore to purchase food for tonight and in the morning. When he returns have the food stored and set about preparing a meal for all those aboard. Mister Powell and I will have whatever you prepare in the cabin."

"Aye," Honest answered.

"But before we consider food, let us get below to have a closer look at the pumps."

"Aye, I'll fetch the lanterns," Honest said.

The first pump was useless. Something inside was jammed and the crank was missing. The second pump had a crank but it turned too freely. The third pump appeared to have been hacked several times with an axe and its pulley and chain were exposed.

"These are useless and it will take days if not weeks to repair," Honest said.

"Mischief knows no bounds nor does laziness," Donland said with disgust.

"Sir, I think I can repair that middle pump in a day if I can go ashore and obtain the parts," Honest stated.

"Then that will be your first chore of the new day," Donland said and added, "The sooner we've pumped her then the sooner we can know what state she is in. Take what men you need and I'll bear the cost of repairing the pumps. Perhaps two pumps will suffice."

"Aye," Honest acknowledged.

Powell sat across from Donland as they ate plates of beans and salt pork.

"Poor fare," Powell said while chewing a piece of the tough pork.

"Aye, but we've a home," Donland mused.

Brunson set down his glass of port and looked from Powell to Donland. "She's a grand lady when she's well commanded and crewed. Captain Shaw, until age and sickness overcame him, was a fair and diligent captain. He was not adverse to dealing harshly with malefactors but a man serving under him was treated fairly."

Powell pursued the thought that was in his mind. "I'd not met Captain Shaw and I believe him to be as you said. How was he at the last?"

Brunson lifted the bottle of port and refilled his glass.

Powell and Donland knew the purpose of refilling was to give time to frame his answer.

Brunson sipped and answered the question. "In the last months there was little doubt that the captain was not the man he once was. He was given to coughing spells and often spit blood into his handkerchief. Mister Marlow, our first assumed more and more responsibility until one day Captain Shaw seemed to grow stronger. The coughing fits subsided but it was apparent that he still was not himself. He ordered floggings for minor infractions, his fairness and good nature gave way to fits of anger. During the last four weeks of his life he ordered us to half-rations but allowed the men double their grog. We've no vegetables or fruits and the men began to wither. Mister Marlow begged the captain to allow us to put to shore and take on fruits but the captain would have none of it. I believe that is why so many men became sick and the fever came upon them. The captain died as we were coming into the roads and Commodore Pettibone had to deal with what to do with *Oxford*. We weren't scheduled to be careened or refitted."

Donland's eyes widened and he asked, "Then why in God's name was her company abandoned and she left sitting here to rot?"

Brunson did not hesitate with his answer, "Only the commodore knows!"

"Then I shall inquire when I see him tomorrow!"

Powell asked, "I should like to attend, may I do so?"

"Aye," Donland answered.

Donland rose from his chair. "Tomorrow we begin pumping her dry. Mister Brunson you and the midshipmen will supervise. Those men not needed on the pumps will be engaged in restoring the rigging. While that is being accomplished, Mister Powell will inspect stores, cordage and sail. Then we will go ashore and confer with Commodore Pettibone about preparing *Oxford* and supplying us with necessary stores."

"I've heard that *Intrepid* is due for a refit and if she is, then she will have preference over *Oxford*." Bunson stated.

"She's not arrived and until has, we will do all we can to see to *Oxford's* needs. And if a careening and a refit are needed, we will be prepared. The decision, however, still lies with the commodore. If we are ready, I do not believe he will deny us. So the next few days are crucial."

Chapter Four

Donland shifted his sword and was about to pick up his hat when there was a tapping at the door. "Come!" he called.

Hornsby entered with his hat under his arm. "Signal from the commodore, *Captain repair ashore.*"

"He's up and about early," Donland said and added, "Call away the gig if you please Mister Hornsby."

"Aye, Captain," Hornsby answered and turned for the door.

"Trouble?" Honest asked.

Donland considered the question and put on his hat. "I think not, he'll know I've had a conversation with Mister Brunson and will want to explain himself and advise me."

"Perhaps," Honest said.

"Yes, perhaps," Donland said as he opened the cabin door. "I shall attend him and see what he intends."

"There's the parts for the pumps, now is as good a time as any to fetch them. I'll set Simon to make and mend in the cabin, there's yet washing to do."

Donland turned, "Aye, you may as well go across but as to Simon, he should be about a man's work with men. Have him report to Mister Brunson."

25

"Aye," Honest answered with a bit of reluctance.

"He'll not grow into man otherwise," Donland said and started for the door.

Fishermen were already on the water and dropping their nets. Other small boats were plying between the merchantmen and the quays. The *Marlin*, a sloop of sixteen guns under the command of Commander Riley lay at anchor several chains from the thirty-two gun frigate, *Orpheus*.

The sun was well into the sky and the coolness of the morning was on the verge of giving way to the heat of the day. The gig scooted across the water toward the wharf. Neither Donland no Powell spoke of weather or other matters on the crossing, as they were each locked in their own thoughts. The boat soon bumped alongside the quay and was steadied by one of the hands. Donland rose and said to the boat's crew, "Wait on the quay, We will not be ashore very long."

Powell dutifully followed Donland onto the quay and to Pettibone's residence.

The clerk said to Donland, "He's waiting for you, Lieutenant Powell should remain outside."

"There's no reason Lieutenant Powell should not be privy to what is said," Donland replied.

"His orders sir, he saw you coming across."

Donland only nodded as the clerk rose from his chair. Powell removed his hat and sat on the bench, "I'll be here," he said.

Pettibone did not rise as Donland entered but did say, "It's too early to offer you refreshments but I've water if you would care for a glass."

"I think not," Donland replied and waited.

"Sit and I will get to the matter at hand," Pettibone said and slid some documents into a desk drawer. "What I've to say is to go no further than this office. I will not ask you to agree but I believe you will do so of your own volition, *Oxford*, as you may have guessed, was not scheduled for careening or refitting. My reports to Admiral Pigot indicated that she was in need of attention. I did not specify the type of attention and he and his staff drew their own conclusions, hence her sitting more or less derelict. You are well familiar with the adage, *for the good of the service?*"

"Aye," Donland answered.

Pettibone continued, "Captain Shaw was held in high esteem by those rank and those of peerage. A black mark against his name would not have been well received and the one doing so would suffer consequences."

"That person being you," Donland interjected.

Pettibone's face reddened but he said flatly, "Yes."

"For the good of the service," Donland repeated the phrase.

"Aye, and my career," Pettibone confessed. "As to the circumstances," he continued. "Captain Shaw had lost his faculties and was incapable of command. His second in command was an ill-mannered and cruel man not worthy of his station. I was, therefore, forced to take action without consulting Admiral Pigot or his staff. As I said, those of peerage would not have taken kindly to disparaging Shaw. The admiral would not have received a report from me stating the facts and truth with any degree of favorability."

"I would think not," Donland said, as he understood Pettibone's difficulty. "Such a report would have kindled the admiral's anger against you for placing him in the position of having to do or say something distasteful. You in fact were saving him from incurring the wrath of others."

"Aye, so you understand why I acted the way I have and why Lieutenant Powell is not privy to our conversation. That being said, Captain Shaw, God rest his soul, has his good name and I my career."

Donland pursed his lips, sat silent for a moment then asked, "You have told me the why, perhaps you will tell me the how for if I am to proceed I think it would be beneficial to know what the implications of your actions will be to my career?"

Pettibone smiled a tight-lipped smile and answered, "The how was not that difficult. The reductions ordered by the Admiralty came at an opportune time. Those worthy of assignment were taken aboard other vessels and those not were discharged or put ashore on half pay. As for *Oxford*, she sits."

"Those on half pay include Shaw's first?"

"Aye, and he is now somewhere aboard an American merchantman, a slaver I believe. You'll have nothing to fear from that quarter."

"And *Oxford*?"

Pettibone scratched his chin. "She's under my orders."

"And when she is ready for sea, what then?"

"She will be ready for sea when I say she is ready for sea, if I ever do. And that, depends on you and Admiral Pigot. I'll not go against his wishes and I'll not have you as captain until you are confirmed. So, I've time to allow her to sit as she is."

Donland felt the anger rising. He pushed it down and was about to object but Pettibone continued.

"Isaac, I'm a fair man and it would be unfair of me to do nothing or not to assist you in readying *Oxford* for sea. I will provide you with what you need but I ask that you bide your time. All does not have to be accomplished in a week or even weeks as we are not at war. You have a command and in a few months all this will be in the past. Accept what you have and prepare for what is to come."

"What of Lieutenant Powell?" Donland asked.

Pettibone's face soured and he said, "I can't assign him to *Oxford* without incurring the admiral's anger. But I can secure him as my flag lieutenant and send you Lieutenant Halston. In this way he will be available to you. It will all be done on paper of course and only you, Captain Hood and I will be privy to it. All others need not know and Powell will be available to you as you need him."

Donland understood what was being offered, he liked none of it. The silence grew heavy as he weighted the matter. Finally, he said, "Lieutenant Powell, I'm sure, will content himself with serving as your flag lieutenant and Lieutenant Halston will learn my ways and methods. I'd rather all be above board rather than at some latter day sink. Is this agreeable to you?"

Pettibone smiled, "It is."

Powell was still on the bench when Donland emerged from Pettibone's office. "Let us return," Donland said and waited as Powell stood.

Powell dutifully followed Donland from the building. He could wait no longer and asked, "What did you learn?"

Donland turned to him and said, "Not here, we will walk for a bit."

They walked along the avenue until they were out of earshot of anyone. Donland said, "It was not as I hoped but it can't be helped. You are to be the commodore's flag officer, employed but not aboard a ship. It was the best I could do."

"And Halston?" Powell asked.

"He will come aboard *Oxford*."

"Aye," Powell said somewhat deflated. He asked, "And *Oxford*?"

"She's not to see the careening wharf, it was a ruse to dispose of her company. I'll not go into details but suffice it to say, the commodore was candid with me and I am with you. In time, *Oxford* will put to sea and you will be first but until then we will bide our time. Commodore Pettibone assures me *Oxford* will be provided for and with you as his flag, you'll be in position to lend aid."

"Then we are both employed and will once again wreak havoc on the high seas," Powell joked.

"Aye, all in time," Donland said and laughed.

Powell became serious and asked, "How long?"

Donland blew a long breath, "That I do not know," Pettibone said "as long as it takes for my confirmation to arrive. I make that to be at least two months and may be as long as six. Until we are needed or until the confirmation we will do our best to keep the company occupied and *Oxford* as operational as possible. I would that you did not speak of this to anyone. If our people inquire, the answer will be that we await orders."

"Aye, I just pray it is the lesser of months for being a clerk is not to my liking but to gain the berth I'll use pen and ink like it is powder and shot. Each stoke will count!"

The boat was not at the quay when they returned. The marine sentry informed Donland that Honest had returned loaded parts for the pumps and departed for *Oxford*.

"He said that you would approve as you wanted the pumps repaired above all else. Shall I call a boat for you, Sir?" the sentry asked.

"No, I'll hire a boat," Donland answered.

The marine signaled to one of the nearby bumboats and two boys rowed the small boat to the quay. Donland and Powell climbed down.

"*Oxford*," Donland said and gave the boys two pennies.

"Aye Captain," the taller of the two boys said in his best naval imitation. The boy was no more than twelve.

The boys were spindly but strong for their size. They crossed the distance to *Oxford* in about the same time that two experienced men would have done so.

David was waiting as Donland came through the sally port. "Honest is working on the pumps and Lieutenant Brunson is below with a party sorting out the cable tier. Mister Hornsby is yonder in the bow supervising the bowsprit party."

"And you?" Donland asked.

"I have the watch," David answered.

"Aye," Donland replied and added, "I shall go below to check on the progress with the pumps. Keep watch for signals from the commodore."

"Aye, Captain," David answered.

To Donland's surprise, Simon was not with his father. Two men were assisting Honest as they dismantled the damaged pump.

"Progress, Honest," Donland asked.

"Aye, we'll have this one ready in an hour. The other by noon, will there be more men to man them?"

"No, we few have it to ourselves. Carry on," Donland said and continued forward toward the cable tier.

"Haul!" Brunson said.

Six men began hauling on the spare anchor cable.

"Easy there!" Brunson called. "Careful of the lad's legs!"

It occurred to Donland that the lad was Simon, he was the one inside the cable tier. He smiled as he remembered telling Honest, *a man to do a man's work.*

"Lieutenant Brunson," Donland said to the man's back.

"Haul!" Brunson said again and men began walking backwards dragging the cable.

Brunson turned. "Beg pardon Captain," he managed. "A tangle an octopus couldn't unknot."

"Keep at it, hopefully you'll have it sorted by the time the pumps are repaired."

"Aye, Captain!"

Donland went up the hatchway to his cabin. He was pleased to see that it had been set to rights except for replacing the glass in the transom. He would set Honest to having it done. The sailcloth was neatly folded and stuffed under the port side long nine's barrel. Judging from the smoke on the overhead deck beams he assumed that the anchor watch had broken up the gun's coverings and burned them in a brazier. The hands will not take pleasure in scrubbing and sanding away the smoke stains.

He saw the lock was broken on the trunk containing the ship's logs and accounts. Lifting the lid he was appalled to see the crumbled papers and torn ledgers. The inside of the trunk smelled of piss. He closed the lid, it would have to be removed and burned.

His trunk contained his personal logs and he would use one of them to record today's activities. Later, David could copy the accounts into a new ship's log. It would be better to start fresh.

An hour passed before a tapping at the door interrupted him. "Come!" he called.

"Beg pardon, Captain, Mister Brunson asks that you come on deck," the young man said.

"Aye, I'll come. What is your name?"

"Hendricks, Captain, able seaman."

Donland put away his log and locked the trunk. He jammed on his hat and went to see why Brunson needed him.

A newcomer was on deck, a lieutenant. Donland had expected him to be Halston but the man wore a marine's' coat. The coat and hat appeared to be new and he sported a rather long queue down his back.

"Captain Donland may I present Lieutenant Sharpe, Royal Marines. He requests he and his men be allowed to board."

Donland peered over the side and saw a dozen marines in two boats. Turning back to Sharpe he asked, "Delighted to make your acquaintance Mister Sharpe, have you orders?"

"The pleasure is mine and I am pleased to be under your command. As to orders, I've not as I and my men are carried on the muster. We served under Captain Shaw."

Donland was at a loss. He had understood from Commodore Pettibone that all of *Oxford's* company had been dispatched to other vessels. "Bring them aboard and report to me in my cabin," he said and turned for the cabin.

"Aye Captain," Sharpe said to Donland's back.

Sharpe appeared at Donland's cabin fifteen minutes later with a tall thick sergeant by the name of Hawkes.

"Sit," Donland said after Sharpe introduced Hawkes. He asked, "How is it that you were separated from the ship and now return?"

Sharpe answered with a hint of bitterness, "The provost, Lieutenant Almonds, ordered us ashore after the captain's funeral. My men and I have been living hand to mouth while guarding warehouses. This morning when I heard old *Oxie* had a new captain I gathered my lads and hired the boats."

Donland tried not to smile. "Came through the hawser?" he asked.

Sharpe flushed with either anger or embarrassment, Donland knew not which.

"Aye, Captain," Sharpe said and stuck out his chin.

Donland liked the young man. Hawkes gave nothing away.

"The provost may well seek you," Donland said.

"Aye, I'm certain he will and that is why I did not seek him out before coming aboard. Someone said that is better to ask forgiveness than to ask permission. I choose to ask your forgiveness Captain Donland and allow us to do our duty to our ship."

"How long were you aboard *Oxford?*" Donland asked.

"I came aboard as a lad some six years ago. Sergeant Hawkes a year before, he was my sergeant."

"I must admit to being curious as to your promotion but that in its own time. For now, I am pleased to have you aboard and I will have a word with Lieutenant Almonds and with the commodore. Settle your men in, set two sentries at the sally port and one at my door. The remainder will have a task that may not be to their liking but is necessary. Report back to me in half an hour."

Sharpe nodded and answered, "Aye, Captain!"

Honest was on his knees pounding a piece of metal with a hammer. The clanking of the nearest pump offset the hammering.

"Almost finished Captain, she'll work like new," Honest said as he wiped sweat.

Donland asked, "What of the other?"

"Dried out bushings is all, I'll soak em' over night and by morning they'll soften and be ready to go back in. All three pumps and the wash pump will have her dry as a baby's bottom in two days."

"Do you require anything?" Donland asked.

Honest stood. "My grog ration would not come amiss," he said and grinned.

"Aye, I shall see to it as I expect the others are as thirsty as you."

Donland sought out David. The young man was filthy. "Sir," David said when he looked up and saw Donland.

"You've been in the hog pen?" Donland asked.

David glanced down at his pants, he had removed his coat. "I slipped while helping move a barrel of pork," David answered.

"Wallowing with the pigs then Mister Welles?" Donland asked with a smile.

The young man did not laugh.

"Go wash and change out of that muck. We've no grog aboard and the men will want their ration. I will prepare a draft for you to present to the clerk at the warehouse, choose two men to attend you." As an afterthought he added, "A Lieutenant Sharpe has come aboard with our complement of marines, have him assign two men to accompany you."

David wiped his hands on his shirt and replied, "Aye, Captain!"

Chapter Five

David selected two men, Watson and Grissom who were near his own age. Lieutenant Sharpe sent along two men named Kingsley and Portman who were considerably older than David. He minded not the ages for he had grown accustomed to supervising those many years his senior.

"They'll not need muskets, they'll help man the boat," David said to Lieutenant Sharpe.

"Bayonets then, just for their own protection," Sharpe said with a wink.

David sat aft in the boat while the four men manned the oars. He was aware that the four knew each other and the banter was light-hearted. The older two teased the two younger ones about their lack of facial hair.

"Old Betty over yonder at the Lion and Lamb pub has more hair on her chin than the two of you together," Portman said.

David instinctively put his hand to his cheek then pretended to rub it as if irritated.

Grissom replied to the taunt, "You need all that bristle to hide your mug!"

They reached the quay and David bounded out of the boat. "Where is the warehouse?" He asked.

"Building just yonder," Portman answered.

David led the way, the door was open, so he entered. A Midshipman sat at a table flipping a knife onto the tabletop. The man appeared to be in his late twenties. David thought to himself that the man was old to be a midshipman.

He proceeded to the table followed by his four men. The midshipman looked up but did not rise or put away the knife.

"What'd you want?" the man sneered.

David had seen his like before and was not intimidated. "I've a draft for a barrel of grog for the *Oxford*." He pulled the draft from his coat.

"The clerk will be back in an hour or so, piss off, don't trouble me with it, it's his job!"

David took the man's words and demeanor in stride. "Your name sir?" David asked.

The man tossed the knife from his left to his right hand and pointed it at David then said, "My name is of no consequence to the likes of you. You best take your draft and shove it where the sun don't shine if you know what's good for you."

Anger rose in David. In one swift move his hand shot forward, grasped the older man's wrist holding the knife and yanked the man's face onto the table. In the next instant his left hand banged the man's head against the table. "The likes of me!" David said as the anger cooled, "Will not tolerate the likes of you!"

"Sir!" Grissom said in a concerned tone to David's back.

David turned and asked, "What is it?"

Grissom leaned forward and whispered, "He'll not forget, sir."

"I'll bloody kill you!" the injured man said as he rose from the table with the knife in his hand. He lunged at David. David jumped back and the blade caught only air as the table was between the two.

David half turned and pulled the bayonet from Portman's belt and sidestepped before the midshipman could thrust.

A hand caught David's shoulder, he shook it off and said to the injured man while jabbing with the bayonet, "I'll not kill you for I'll not hang but blast your soul, I'll leave you crippled!"

Shock appeared on the man's face as he jumped back from David's jab.

"Take that from him before I kill him, by gawd I will!" The man shouted to those behind David.

No one spoke but each man did take a step back.

"I'll report this to the provost, he'll have you up on charges!" The man shouted again.

The anger and fighting madness left David. He eyed the old midshipman and shook his head as if to say, *you're a sorry lot and not worth the sweat.*

He handed the bayonet back to Portman and said, "You men remain here while I seek out the provost. Don't let him leave."

"Aye, sir," Portman answered.

David started for the door and Portman came alongside. "Beg pardon, sir," Portman said, "but the provost and that one are mates. It'll do no good to get him, and it'll do no good to piss on that one."

David understood but kept walking. Portman stayed by his side. Once outside David turned to Portman, "Thank you for your advice and cool head. I shouldn't have let him goad me."

"Aye, but you'd not know his sort," Portman said. "I've dealings with him before, he sells the grog he steals. The provost knows and gains coin from the dealings. We best leave him and wait for the clerk to return."

David weighted the advice and considered what he should do. He knew he was too junior to make accusations and he cared not to anger the man further. He turned to Portman, "Fetch the others and wait for me at the quay. I will return with the barrel."

"Sir?" Portman asked.

"Do as I order, there's no need to fear for me for I've a friend that will aid me."

"Aye, sir," Portman answered.

David asked the clerk sitting in the foyer for Lieutenant Powell.

"Your name and reason for seeing Lieutenant Powell?" The tall balding clerk asked.

"An invitation to dine with Captain Donland," David lied.

The clerk nodded and said, "Second door on the right."

The door was open and David tapped at the facing.

Powell was sitting at a desk making entries into a log. He looked up and smiled. "Mister Welles this is unexpected."

David half-turned and closed the door. The windows were open so David came close to the desk before saying, "Beg pardon for my intrusion, may I have a word?"

Powell stood, "Aye, it sounds as if there is trouble."

"Aye," David said.

Powell came around the desk to David and asked, "The nature of this trouble?"

David came out with it. "I'm tasked with obtaining a barrel of grog from the warehouse for *Oxford*. I encountered a midshipman there, an older man perhaps mid-twenties. The clerk was not there and when I presented the draft for the grog, he was belligerent and threatened me with a knife. I managed to avoid his swipe and banged his head against the table. He then threatened me with the provost who one of my men informed me, was the man's friend and together they were robbing the warehouse and selling the supplies. My concern is the grog, the other I've no mind to pursue."

Powell responded, "That is a serious charge and the midshipman's actions are a hanging offense. Why come to me?"

David said again, "As I said, I came only for the grog, the other I care not to pursue. As a favor to me, would you return with me to the warehouse?"

Powell considered for a moment then said, "Aye, I'll come, wait for me outside the warehouse. Our meeting will appear as happenstance."

"Aye," David answered.

David did as Powell ordered. He found his men and returned to the door of the warehouse. Their wait was short and when Powell appeared at the door he said to David, "Mister Welles how is it with you?"

David went along with the charade, "I am well and you, sir?"

"Very well, and your Captain?"

"He sends his regards should I encounter you," David said and entered the warehouse with Powell at his side. To his surprise there was another officer, a lieutenant.

Powell continued with David to the table where the midshipman was standing and the lieutenant off to one side. "Is the storekeeper about?" Powell asked.

"He's away at present and I am standing in until he returns," the midshipman stated.

Powell turned to David and said, "I believe Mister Welles has a transaction to make before we return to the commodore's office."

David pulled the draft from his pocket as if he had not been there before.

"I'm for a barrel of grog for *Oxford*," David said to the midshipman.

The midshipman looked from the lieutenant to Powell then back to David. He took the draft from David's hand.

The other officer said to Powell, "You are aquatinted with the midshipman, er Welles isn't it?"

Powell smiled, "Aye, we've served together, Mister Almonds, he is Captain Donland's ward and serves aboard *Oxford*. A fine young officer if I'm to judge."

Almonds did not reply.

"Grog is yonder," the old midshipman said.

"Aye," David replied and started in the direction indicated. The two seaman and two marines followed. Grissom elbowed Watson.

Powell did not follow them from the warehouse.

The barrel was loaded into the boat and David sat on the rear seat. The four men rowed and made jabs at one another about drinking, women and cards. The incident in the warehouse was not mentioned. David had no doubts it would be told and exaggerated below deck. Honest would surely hear and relay it to Donland. He decided he would have to tell Donland himself.

Chapter Six

Donland was not amused. David's account was the facts, stated exactly as he would have had he faced the knife. He wanted to put it down as the foolishness of youth but knew it was more than that. David had stood his ground, what a man would have done, and for that he felt pride. But he felt more pride in that David used his head to accomplish his task by seeking out Powell.

He chose his words with care. "I would that you do not enter the town again without another officer present. You were fortunate to take him with surprise, but his kind does not forget. Nor will he be long in seeking an opportunity to cause you harm. Should you go about the town with Simon, he will chose Simon as his target in order to get at you. Better that you be in the company of Mister Brunson, Lieutenant Sharpe or even Mister Hornsby and even then he will have support from others."

David shifted his weight uncomfortably in the chair. He was about to speak but Donland put a finger to his lips.

A deck plank overhead had given a loud squeak.

Donland came from around the desk and leaned forward. "I'm proud of you, you know you are like a brother to me, and I'd not want you harmed. I can accept you in danger when the guns grind down the ship and boarders slash and thrust while you fight for your life. But, my anger is kindled hot when the likes of that bastard threaten you. In doing so he has made an enemy he will come to fear. Now, I will say no more of this nor will you. I've a list for the port storekeeper and I am sending Lieutenant Brunson with a party of twelve men ashore, you are to accompany him. No doubt you will encounter that midshipman again, do not be goaded!"

David met Donland's eyes, "Aye, Captain, I will not but I'll not be insulted."

"Nor do I expect you to accept such. My concern is that you will not let your heart overwhelm your head."

"Aye," David said.

Honest entered the cabin without tapping at the door. He was covered in grime and sweat. "The pumps are repaired and Mister Hornsby is setting some of the men to pump. I'll have my grog and wash up."

"Well done, once we have her dry we can get on with repairs that will surely be needed," Donland said then asked, "What of Simon?"

"He's about," Honest said.

Tapping at the doorframe announced Lieutenant Sharpe.

"Beg pardon Captain," he said and then seeing Honest added, "I can wait."

"No need Mister Sharpe, my coxs'un was leaving. You've come about the task I have for you?"

"Aye, Sir."

"Will you have a glass? I've some brandy," Donland offered.

"Thank you kindly Captain, but no, I'm not a drinking man."

"Then to the matter," Donland said and sat in his chair with the transom windows to his back. "Had we a full company I'd not ask you to take on the task, but as we are so few, I've little choice. We've more than our share of vermin aboard. In the months *Oxford* has languished, she has become overrun. I would that your men kill the buggers. Use whatever means you prefer, start wherever you choose but rid us of as many as possible."

Sharpe grinned and offered, "A suggestion, Captain, perhaps you would care to award a prize to the man who kills the most. The lads would take to the task if there were a prize to be had."

"A little sport and wagers on the side," Honest said with understanding.

"Aye, they'd relish it and we'd rid ourselves of more vermin."

Donland considered the suggestion. "One week time limit and you will verify each kill and Sergeant Hawkes will dispose of the killed rats. A guinea and a night ashore will be sufficient prize, what say you?"

Sharpe replied, "Were I not an officer and a gentleman, I'd be keen to take it on."

"Such is our lot Mister Sharpe, we miss the thrill of the hunt."

"Aye, Captain," Sharpe said and added, "The lads will be eager to get at em' to gain the prize."

A tapping at the door interrupted them. A rather rotund man with a cherub face stood awkwardly. Donland noted the lieutenant's coat and said, "Enter Mister Halston."

"I will be about my duties Captain if you have no need of me," Sharpe said.

"Aye, Lieutenant Sharpe," Donland said and in the next breath, "Welcome aboard Lieutenant Halston, close the door and we shall get aquatinted." Nervously Halston managed, "Yes, Sir."

Honest also excused himself, "I'm for my grog," he said and followed Sharpe.

"Care for a glass of brandy?" Donland asked Halston as he moved to the sideboard.

"Thank you. Perhaps it will settle my stomach, I fear I've ingested something that refuses to settle."

Donland poured two glasses. As he did, he considered how he was to make use of the nervous man that was to be first officer. He handed a glass to Halston and asked, "Does your stomach trouble you often?"

Halston answered, "On occasion, yes, well that is, uncertainty unsettles me in general."

Donland smiled and lifted his glass, "Brandy is good for the stomach so I've been told and have found it to be so. Small amounts mind you."

"Ah, yes, I've heard. A surgeon said something similar to me when I went aboard my first ship."

"And what was that?" Donland asked.

"The *Atropos*, that was some ten years ago."

Donland moved behind his desk and sat. He said to Halston, "Sit if you please."

The chair was plain without upholstery and one leg had been mended with a piece of planking. Halston eyed if as if it were too frail for his girth. He said, "Perhaps I should stand, if you don't mind."

"There's another just behind you, I believe it to be more comfortable than the other," Donland said indicating the chair with his hand.

Halston turned, seemed to gauge the strength of the chair then picked it up and sat it next to the repaired one. He then picked up the repaired chair and placed it where the other had sat.

Somewhat annoyed, Donland sat patiently and sipped the brandy. The man would never do as first officer. Pettibone would have known Halston's shortcomings. No doubt Pettibone wanted Halston away from him for a time.

Halston sat, fumbled with his hat and finally stood and put the hat on the corner of Donland's desk. As he was about to sit he stopped. Looked at his hat then crossed to the desk, retrieved the hat and placed it on the sideboard.

"Mister Halston sit!" Donland barked.

Halston sat and his face turned bright red.

Donland drained his glass, rose and refilled it. He realized in an instant that having Halston aboard would tax his energies. He studied the man for a moment. Drank a gulp of brandy and studied Halston again for a long moment. He then asked, "Mister Halston has Commodore Pettibone explained to you that *Oxford* is going to remain as she is for some time?"

Halston looked up at Donland and answered, "He has, she's not to put to sea until orders from Admiral Pigot are sent."

"Then, let me outline your duties. You will serve as our purser and master. Your duties will be confined to ordering, inventory, and maintaining logs. I shall not burden you with tasks above deck other than watch keeping. Is that suitable to you?"

The rotund man's eyes widened and he stammered, "Yes, yes that would be most suitable."

Donland smiled, "Very well then, it shall be as I've stated. Mister Brunson will see to the needs above deck and you below deck until we receive orders. Then, I believe Commodore Pettibone will desire you continue in his service. Give my compliments to Lieutenant Brunson, when he comes back aboard and have him prepare you a cabin."

"Will he be coming aboard soon?" Halston asked.

"Soon Mister Halston, wait for him on deck. I've matters to attend so you are excused."

"Thank you Captain, my mind and my stomach are settling. As I said, uncertainty is troublesome."

"That is all Mister Halston, go wait for Mister Brunson's return. He will have a list of stores he's received from the storekeeper.

Halston rose and looked for his hat, recovered it from the sideboard and made it to the door before looking back. Donland was purposely holding up a ledger to the transom windows.

"Sentry!" Donland called once Halston was away.

The door opened and the marine with heavy graying long sideburns entered.

"Suh!" the marine said as he entered.

"And you are?" Donland asked.

"Private Heartshaw, suh!"

"See that I am not disturbed, no one and I mean no one less than commodore rank is to darken my door!"

The marine grinned and replied, "Aye, suh!"

Donland thought the marine was going to grin and wink. The man had heard every word of the conversation with Halston, he would be telling it to his mates over grog.

"One thing Heartshaw, do not speak of my conversation with Lieutenant Halston to anyone. I can assure that if you do, I will know and you'll not enjoy your duty aboard this vessel! Do you understand?"

"Aye, suh, the rats will have it better than me."

Donland grinned, "Aye, they will. That's all."

"Suh!" Heartshaw grinned then turned on his heel.

The brandy made Donland's head spin and he chose to lie down on his cot. There was no enemy and there was nothing to claim his attention on deck. His time in Port Royal was to be endured much like a prison sentence. Pettibone had made that much clear.

If that was to be the case, he was determined to be at ease as much as possible. *Oxford's* needs would be met and on the day she was called to go forth, she would be ready and so would he. There was a letter to be written, he had put it off but now he had no excuse. Betty Sumerford would be waiting for the letter, perhaps as much as he longed for another from her. The last letter he had received was before being assigned to act as guide for *Brune's* misadventure. The letter was lost when *Brune* went under as were the other letters from her that he had cherished and kept. Writing her would wait a bit longer. Suddenly, he yawned.

He entered the stateroom, removed his boots and lay down on the cot. The faint lapping of the waves against the hull combined with the ever so slight rocking of the ship were all that were needed for him to begin to drift off to sleep. The singsong squeak of planking was his lullaby.

He dreamed that Betty had taken a room at an inn. He went to visit her on a moonlit night. There, on a balcony, in the moonlight they embraced. It was the last image in his head before he was awakened.

"Captain!" Honest called rousing Donland from deep sleep. "It's nigh on sunset!" Honest stated. Instantly he raised up and in one motion wheeled himself around, his stocking feet hitting the deck.

"Brandy," he managed.

"Aye, I'll fetch you a glass," Honest said.

"Belay, it was the brandy I drank earlier. Blasted drink!"

Honest laughed.

"My boots," Donland said as he felt for them.

Honest watched as Donland slipped on his boots and when he felt Donland was reasonably attentive he reported, "Mister Brunson and Mister Welles returned with the stores. There was no trouble ashore like before. Mister Powell sent word by Mister

Brunson that as flag lieutenant, that there will be those that get their comeuppance. I'd not want to be in their boots."

"Aye," Donland said as he stood. "Mister Powell will sort them." Then asked, "What of Lieutenant Halston?"

Honest grinned as he held out Donland's coat. "Ledgers and papers instead of sails and yards. Mister Brunson wasn't taken with him."

"I would think not, I'd empty the brandy were I with him more than an hour."

Honest laughed again, "Can't have that!"

"No we can't," Donland agreed.

The sound of a pistol shot reached Donland's ear. "What the blazes was that?"

"The marines," Honest said. "One of the lads told me he was going to win the prize. Seems Mister Sharpe has given them permission to hunt rats and given them pistols. They are to use half charges and split balls so as not to cause damage. He said you will pay the prize for the most killed in the week."

"Aye," Donland agreed. "Seemed reasonable at the time but I'd not bargained for hunting with pistols. Perhaps I should put an end to it."

"Best not Captain, the lads would be disappointed and Lieutenant Sharpe has laid down rules. No pistols on the gun deck and only baited rats can be shot."

"Baited rats?" Donland asked.

"Aye, a bit of cheese or bread laid out where the rat can get at it and the lad has a clear shot."

"There's the magazine, has he considered that!"

"Aye, sir. We've no power aboard, I've been in the magazine, still a bit of water in there but I managed. Empty barrels is all."

"That's a comfort for now, were it not for the peace I'd not sleep having no powder aboard."

A heavy knock at the door ended the conversation. "See to it while I wash my face," Donland said to Honest.

Donland was drying his face when Honest called, "Mister Brunson, Captain," Honest called from beyond the partition.

"Aye, I'll come," Donland answered as he pulled back his thick black hair and tied it with the black ribbon Betty had given him.

"Beg pardon Captain, I've come about a couple of matters," Brunson began.

"Aye, I expect you've a few bearing on you," Donland said as he sat in his chair. Pray have a seat Mister Brunson.

"I'll have your dinner before long," Honest said.

Brunson waited until he heard Honest clattering about preparing Donland's meal. "First, I can report that the troublesome midshipman, Marston, was not present when I went to the warehouse. Mister Welles relayed the previous encounter as we were going across. The storekeeper was quite helpful when I arrived. I did keep Mister Welles occupied inside with me while the stores were sorted. I trust my actions were to your liking?"

"Aye, and as I would have done," Donland said.

"What of Mister Halston?" Brunson asked.

Donland ran his fingers through his still damp hair and said "Lieutenant Halston will be with us for as long as we are tied to the land. His duties will be confined below deck. I will be looking to you for all else. Such an arrangement of duties, I believe, will serve our people and set *Oxford* to rights."

Brunson pursed his lips.

"Have you a thought?" Donland asked.

"We've myself, Hornsby and Mister Welles will there be another coming aboard?"

"No, not until we have orders from the admiral. As to watches, Lieutenant Halston is to have his turn. I would ask that you set the watches, since we are at anchor the midshipmen may stand theirs independently. Have we a master's mate?"

"No, Sir, not even a bos'um. Your cox'sun is senior. But I've a man in mind that would make a fair bos'um, his name is Stewart."

"I shall leave that in your hands if that is agreeable with you?"

"Aye, Captain, it is and I will apprise Lieutenant Powell of my choice if that pleases you?"

"Thank you for that, Mister Brunson, I would that we keep Mister Powell apprised of such matters. His being ashore with paper and pen will be a punishment."

"Aye, it would be for me, I say better him than me."

Donland smiled and said, "If there are no other matters I will have my dinner, and I would that you and Mister Halston sit with me tomorrow night."

"Aye, Captain," Brunson said and rose from the chair.

Chapter Seven

Corporal Grayson won the prize for killing forty-one rats. The total for the week among the marines was three hundred and ten. The last day of the hunt claimed only two rats. Donland deemed the rat-killing competition to be a success. He did not believe for a moment that all the vermin were eradicated but there would be few remaining.

Oxford's holds were dry, though water still seeped and filled the bilge.

Lieutenant Powell, in his capacity as flag captain, ordered the master carpenter to examine the hull. The man was amazed that he found very little rot and what there was would not hinder *Oxford's* sailing capabilities. It was as good a clean bill of health Donland thought possible. His remaining concern was the amount of weed growing on her bottom. He decided to see for himself.

There were few clouds and the wind was no more than a whisper. Those aboard thought he had lost his mind when he stripped and dove over the side. The water was warm and clear of sediment. He swam the entire larboard length under water, gulped air and submerged again returning to the bow along the starboard side. The weed and barnacles were thick adding a great deal of weight to *Oxford*. She'd not keep pace with ships-of-the-line.

Honest handed Donland a towel after his swim. "How's her bottom?" he asked.

"She needs scraping," Donland answered.

"Aye, I thought as much, she's old and I'd wager she's not been careened in her life."

"Let us go to the cabin, I'll dress and go across to the commodore," Donland said as he briskly rubbed his hair.

He was in the midst of dressing when there sounded a stamping of the marine sentry's boots outside the cabin and then a heavy knock. "Enter!" Donland shouted as he put on his coat.

Powell entered with a smile. "I've heard you had an afternoon swim," he said.

"Aye, wanted to see how much weed was on her bottom, seems a good day for it," Donland said and asked, "Brandy, grog or water?"

"Nothing at this time perhaps later. Let us sit," Powell said.

Donland was keenly aware of Powell's familiarity tone rather than the formal naval stiffness. "You've come as a friend and not as an emissary of the commodore?"

"Aye as a friend. I do want to commend you on what you've managed in two weeks. Were it not for the lack of sail on the masts I would think I were aboard another ship. How is it below deck? Have you plugged her leaks?"

"The leaks were minor, no more than expansion and contraction. New tar and oakum has her as dry as any in the fleet. The pumps are needed only every other day. The rigging is another matter, the rot is far more than I imaged. Every time I go to the storekeeper he tells me that the commodore hasn't approved my requests. It is becoming frustrating. I trust you have come to tell me my requests are approved?"

"No, I've not and if I could, I would see that you have what you requested. Commodore Pettibone is bound by the admiral's orders and he will not circumvent them. However, there may be a changing of the wind before long. I've heard of forced retirements and other changes taking place in London."

"Perhaps Admiral Pigot will be replaced," Donland said.

"Only time will tell," Powell said. "But, the reason for my visit is to inform you that I've ten men for you. I'm sure they will come as a welcome addition?"

"Aye, if they aren't the dregs of some prison."

"They are not that. A boat arrived a few hours ago, how they managed the crossing is a mystery to me other than to assume they had a good teacher."

Donland was curious, "How big of a boat? I've not heard of any vessel entering the roads."

"A fishing boat just large enough for ten men," Powell said while smiling broadly. "The captain asked for you."

"Me? Who is this fellow?"

"He called himself Bill Freedman."

"Bill!" Donland was shocked. "He was to sail with the old *Hornet.*"

"Aye, he did," Powell began to explain. "The *Carolina*, put in at Cockburn Town and the lads deserted. Said they would not sail with a man who disliked their kind. They pooled their money and set out to find you. Curious thing, they said pay or no pay they serve with Captain Donland. For that reason, I'll have them brought aboard as long as you don't carry them on the muster."

Donland was dumbfounded. "They've come all this way in an open boat! Just in hopes that I would provide for them! Unbelievable!"

"Aye, why they would risk so much for you is beyond my understanding. You must feed them well?"

"No more than any others but these are men who were once slaves and you know how they were treated."

"Aye, filthy business, those who engage in it should be put before the gratings," Powell stated then asked, "Do you want them sent across?"

"Aye and am pleased to do so. Such loyalty is to be rewarded."

"True," Powell said. He reached inside his coat and brought out an envelope. "Loyalty, I do wonder how some give it so freely to someone so undeserving."

Donland's eyes were fixed on the envelope. "Betty Sumerford?"

"Why she cares for you is another mystery I can't fathom," Powell said as he handed the envelope across. "And now, I think I've earned a drink."

Donland barely heard and responded, "Aye."

While Powell rose and went to the sideboard, Donland carefully opened the envelope. Unfolding the sheets, his hungry eyes found the salutation, "My love."

Donland stood on his quarterdeck feeling all was right with the world. In his inside breast pocket was the letter, the wind was fair and his company was minding their tasks. Lieutenant Sharpe and Sergeant Hawkes were drilling the marines in close-order. Bill and his mates were in the process of mending and splicing the foremast rigging.

Two other ships of war were anchored in the roads. The seventy-four *High Castle* and the fourteen gun *Specter*. Donland did not know either captain. But was told by Powell that the *High Castle* was to sail for Antigua and the *Specter* would be bound for Bermuda. His *Oxford* would be the only one remaining at Port Royal. As he gazed across the water he was momentarily envious of both captains.

"Captain, boat coming across," Midshipman Welles announced.

"Aye," Donland answered and gave the boat his attention. He saw no officer. Four men pulled the boat and a midshipman sat in the stern. No doubt the boy would be bringing a message.

He pulled his handkerchief from his sleeve, removed his hat and mopped his brow.

"Hour!" Welles announced, turned the glass and rang the bell six times signaling the hour of the afternoon watch. "The glass is turned!"

"Make note in the log," Donland called knowing Welles would have the book out and doing so.

He sighed, he would rather be at sea with a strong wind filling the sails but that would come in time. The sameness of the days waiting for either Pigot to change his mind about *Oxford* or for Pigot to be replaced was to be endured. There was nothing that could be done until one of those two events occurred.

The boat bumped alongside and in seconds. A young boy, no more than eleven, bounded through the sally port. The boy's head swiveled from side to side as if alerted to danger. Donland watched the boy and called to Welles, "Take the youngster in hand Mister Welles!"

"Aye, Captain," David answered and shot past him.

The boat that brought the boy was already making its way back to the quay. The fact that it did so raised Donland's curiosity. Powell had not mentioned a midshipman coming aboard, perhaps he had not known and the decision lay wholly with Commodore Pettibone.

Donland watched as Welles conversed with the youngster and examined a document the boy thrust at him. The boy was not a messenger and his presence could only mean that he was to join the company. The small satchel he carried would contain all his worldly goods.

Welles brought the boy onto the quarterdeck, the boy appeared petrified. Welles made the introduction. "Captain Donland this is Midshipman Oliver Mellencamp lately of the *High Castle*. He is the son of a clergyman in Essex. Commodore Pettibone has entrusted you with his care and training."

"Welcome aboard Mister Mellencamp, Mister Welles will see you to the midshipman's mess and familiarize you with your duties. Do your duty and all will be well with you."

The boy looked up into Donland's face but said nothing. Welles nudged the boy and said to him, "Say, Aye, Captain!"

The boy was at least quick on the mark, "Aye, Captain Donland, Sir!"

Donland could not contain himself; he laughed. Once it passed he said, "We'll not be setting sail for a few weeks, you've time to learn and Mister Welles will be your guide. Mister Hornsby is senior midshipman and will assign you to a watch. Report to him once you've your hammock."

Again the boy stood mute until prodded by Welles, "Aye Captain."

"Aye, Captain!" Mellencamp managed.

Welles took the boy by the elbow and led him to the hatch.

Honest came to Donland's elbow and asked, "Wonder why they wanted rid of the lad?"

"Probably to save someone from hanging," Donland ventured.

"Aye, that would explain it, aye it would."

"Keep a watch on the boy and have Simon befriend him. I'd like to know more about him and how he has come to be with us."

"Simon will be pleased to have another lad aboard, though he and Mister Welles are thicker than thieves and closer than brothers."

Donland nodded and said, "That I know."

Before Honest could ask the question, Donland answered, "Do not be concerned, I've written my request to the commodore for Simon to receive his step. He'll not refuse as I included Simon's valuable aid in freeing Lord Angermanland."

"Thank you kindly," Honest replied and stepped back to the helm.

Hornsby was coming forward from the forecastle. He had witnessed Mellencamp coming aboard. "A new midshipman, Captain?"

"Aye," Donland answered. "Mister Welles has him in tow. He is to report to you and I would accept it kindly if you were to give him a few days to settle. He comes to us from the seventy-four without explanation."

"Without explanation Captain?"

"Aye, I've not been made aware of why but I shall and until then the lad is to be treated with," Donland searched for the word, "shall we say as a guest."

Hornsby's faced screwed up, "A guest, Captain? No duties?"

"Duties yes, but avoid harshness. I fear the lad has received his share. I will, as I said, seek an explanation."

Hornsby sighed and said, "Aye, Captain, I will be mindful of my words. I would that my first captain had been so inclined as you."

"Aye, and mine as well," Donland added.

Hornsby lingered.

"Something Mister Hornsby," Donland asked.

"Sir, any word when we will sail?"

"None Mister Hornsby, none. You, just as I, am employed and for the foreseeable future let us be content with that."

Hornsby smiled, "Aye, Captain, aye. I'd not want to be digging rotten potatoes from the ground."

"Nor, I Mister Hornsby. Return to your duties."

"Aye, Captain," Hornsby answered and left the quarterdeck.

Powell was seated at a table in the inn's dining room. His hat was on the table as was a bottle of wine and two glasses. Donland sat.

"You received my gift?" Powell asked as Donland poured wine into his glass.

"Mister Mellencamp?" Donland asked.

"Aye, Lieutenant Fisher, first on *High Castle* brought him ashore. His captain thought it best that the lad be away from unsavory influences."

"I'm surprised the captain would be concerned?"

Powell lifted his glass and sipped. "I've ordered our dinner, roasted chicken. I trust that will be suitable."

"Aye, it is for you know my tastes. And since I'm your guest, the decision is yours to make. Now, as to the captain's concerns?"

Powell set his glass down. "The vicar's wife, that is the boy's mother, is sister to the captain. Fisher, was aware that the boy was being mistreated and bullied in the midshipman's berth. The usual fare, mind you, nothing more. However, the boy wrote his mother, the mother spoke to the sister and Captain Herriman received a letter from his wife. Fisher, whom I have known since our midshipman days came to me. I explained that *Oxford* was to be in Port Royal for several months and that she was lightly manned and that you had a soft heart and a soft head."

"He becomes my problem," Donland stated.

"Aye, and the lad will write his mother and say that all is well with him and she will tell her sister and she will write Captain Herriman and you will get another promotion."

"Promotion be damned! I want to be at sea!"

Powell laughed then said, "As I do and I took that into consideration before sending you the lad."

"How so?" Donland asked.

"*High Castle* is bound for Antigua and then England. I will leave it to your imagination as to who Captain Herriman's childhood friend and cousin was?"

Donland sat straight up in his chair, "You sly fox! How did you come by that information?"

Powell beamed and said, "Mister Fisher, shared the odd bit, so when he inquired as what to do with the lad, I made the suggestion. I dare say when Herriman sits down to dine with Admiral Pigot, your name will surface and something good will be said about you."

"Let us hope orders to sail will follow," Donland said.

"Aye, every good thing is beneficial is it not?" Powell asked.

"Good deeds deserve rewards, you mean?"

"That too, that too," Powell said as he lifted his glass.

"Still, such a small thing is unlikely to cause the admiral to waver."

"I agree but enough sand can tip the scales."

"Then, let us drink to the sand," Donland said.

Chapter Eight

Oxford settled into a routine of watches, make and mend and pumping over the next three weeks. Port Royal saw only traders and fisherman enter the roads during those weeks. One notable visitor was the packet that brought Donland to Port Royal. He invited Commander Johnson aboard to dine. The young officer accepted and brought news.

"Admiral Pigot has dispatched two sloops to the Falklands. Seems the Dons are kicking up a fuss and have seized some British merchantmen."

"Show and bluster," Donland commented.

"Aye, but as I understand things the Spaniards are being threatened by the Portuguese. Our people are caught in the middle. Might be some fighting, us siding with the Portuguese. I've voyaged there twice and care not to go again but when you are a fleet's messenger you go where ordered."

"That I know well for I've also endured that duty. A thankless and harrowing task," Donland replied as he remembered his first duties when given *Hornet*.

"Any stirrings in London?" Donland asked.

"Aye, heads are still rolling, repercussions of losing the colonies and pressure being applied to those supplying the Frogs with naval stores. A few are being tried for treason to the Crown. And then there is a fellow named Robespierre whipping up cries for a French revolution. Talk is that he is gaining enough support to topple the monarchy. The Whigs in London are watching and praying that old Louie will have Robespierre's head in a basket before he grows strong enough to gain supporters in England."

Donland considered Johnson's suppositions. If what had begun in the American colonies were to spread to the European nations and monarchies were toppled, the entire world would turn upside down and wars would surely break out. He pursed his lips then said, "His head will either be in a basket soon or someone will put a ball through his head. The nobs will not let him continue to espouse rebellion and revolution. They've too much to lose. You can mark it down, he's a dead man on borrowed time."

Johnson smiled at that and said, "Aye, they and us if they don't kill him."

The following week Donland was ordered to Pettibone's office. Powell was in attendance as was the master sail-maker.

After the pleasantries Pettibone announced that he had made a decision as to what is to be done with *Oxford*. "Her sails are stored in the sail loft and I believe it is best to have them sent across and hoisted before the rats consume them. Mister Moss will mend them and send them across."

He turned to Donland, "Are the masts and rigging in order to receive them?"

"Aye, Sir, all standing rigging is repaired and recently tarred. We've repaired and cleaned all blocks and the tackles are like new."

"Have you enough men?" Pettibone asked.

"I've thirty-seven aboard, twenty-seven are on the muster and the other ten are not, do I have your permission to enter them into the muster?"

"Yes, yes, see to it. I believe you will also be requiring a carpenter, mates for him, a sail-maker and a mate for him."

"And a pursuer would not come amiss," Donland stated. "Mister Halston has handled the affairs thus far but if I am to be required to go to sea in the near future, a would that Mister Powell be returned. And that will necessitate a pursuer."

"Yes, I see your point but, I must remind you of my position, all that you require must be put into writing and sent along to Captain Hood. He will not be pleased if I'm seen to be aiding you beyond his instructions."

"Aye, I understand," Donland said and remained hopeful.

Pettibone half-smiled. Picked up a document from his desk and handed it across to Powell. Powell glanced at it and handed it over to Donland who read it and nodded.

"You are in agreement?" Pettibone asked.

"As you order, I will heartily obey."

"Then it is settled, you will have your sails and afterwards we shall consider your other requests," Pettibone said and rose.

The carpenter, a tall Welshman named Blankenship and his two mates, Martin and York arrived that afternoon. They set about inspecting the hull and making notes as to what was to be repaired.

The sail-maker, a small wiry man with hands like leather named Lawson came the following morning with the fore tops'l and fores'l. While the sails were being brought up from the boat by hoist, Lawson inspected the fore mast and the yards. Once returned to the deck he began giving orders. Bill and his mates took to the tasks of rigging the sails with great relish. Everyone aboard sensed the coming change; *Oxford* was coming alive.

Powell came aboard for dinner three days later after the mizzenmast sails were hoisted from the boat. He commented, "Does my heart good to see those and the others. When I first arrived and was told of the situation, I feared that I would be like them, sitting and rotting. Now, perhaps with sails we'll yet feel the sea beneath our heels."

"Aye," Donland agreed. "It is only a matter of time." He changed the topic and announced, "Honest has prepared slabs of roasted beef on the brazier for our dinner. He declares the meat will melt in your mouth like butter after having roasted since early morning."

Powell remarked, "From the smell I would recommend posting an additional sentry. You'll have a rebellion to get at your table."

Donland laughed and answered, "Aye, were it not for the fact that I purchased enough for the company to prepare themselves and a sufficient quantity of wine."

"What? They forfeit their grog?"

"They had their ration but I felt a bit of celebration was in order. They've done more since coming aboard that I dared hope and endured considerable scorn. It is my way of showing appreciation. I thought it best to do so now rather than after we have all our sails hoisted. These lads have earned their reward and I'll not spoil it by including those yet to be added to the muster."

"Aye," Powell said and added. "It is like you to do so, reward the deserving while it can be appreciated." He paused then continued, "When the hail of chain shot rains down and the balls crash like thunder sending shards of wood tearing into flesh they'll remember for whom they fight and die. Not king nor country but for their captain and their mates."

"Well said and to that I would add that glory belongs to the dead and gratitude to the living. Their duty as ours is to our mates. Shall we drink to that?"

"Aye," Powell replied and followed Donland to the sideboard.

A knock at the door and the stamp of feet announced Donland's other guests.

"Enter!" he shouted.

Lieutenant Halston and the midshipmen, Welles, Hornsby and Mellencamp followed Lieutenant Sharpe into the cabin.

"Gentlemen we were about to have a toast, please take a glass and I will pour," Donland invited.

They did as directed and Donland began to pour wine into each glass. Once done he lifted his glass and said, "Glory belongs to the dead and gratitude to the living. Their duty as ours is to our mates!"

"Here! Here!" They replied in unison and drank.

"Gentlemen thank you coming to dine with me tonight. Let us sit and enjoy this evening," Donland said as he moved to his chair.

Each of the men took a chair sitting according to rank with Powell taking the right chair next to Donland and Halston the left. The midshipmen sat at the low end of the table with Hornsby taking the senior chair at the end.

Honest entered and placed two chilled bottles of wine on the table. One he sat in front of Donland and the other in front of Lieutenant Sharpe. Sharpe immediately reached for the bottle and filled his glass. "I propose a toast to Captain Donland, we've not had opportunity to salute him on his promotion, one justly earned."

"Aye," they all answered in unison.

Donland stood as they were passing the bottles and filling glasses. "I think such a toast, though admirable, is premature. Some of you know that my promotion must first be confirmed in London while others here may not know that is the case. Let us not drink that toast and let us reserve it until my confirmation. At that time I promise you that we will again assemble to eat and drink our fill to the point we must be carried from the cabin!"

Sharpe stood, "I amend my toast, let us drink to our Captain's health and to his confirmation!"

They all began to stand and lifted their glasses, "Aye! To Captain Donland!"

Once the wine was downed they sat. Donland remained standing. "I thank you for your toast Lieutenant Sharpe, I do not know about you gentlemen but I have smelled the beef on that brazier all day and I am ravenous." He called, "Honest let us have at it!"

Honest came from behind the curtain with a heavy-laden platter piled high with slabs of roasted beef. Watson also carried a platter, following him was Simon struggling with a platter heaped with boiled potatoes still in their skins.

Those at the table quickly stabbed the slabs of beef and potatoes. Honest returned with two serving dishes piled with carrots.

"There is pudding and custards to follow!" Honest announced as he watched the men and boys heaping their plates with food. None seemed to take notice of the word pudding except for young Mellencamp whose eyes became wide as saucers.

Donland watched them eat, laugh, drink and talk. He did take notice that the youngest midshipman ate very little beef and when the puddings and custards were placed on the table, he was the first to fill his plate.

The question he knew would be coming was finally broached. Sharpe asked, "Captain when will we sail?"

The question stopped all conversation, each man eager for the answer. Mellencamp was not concerned as his mouth was stuffed with another small custard.

Donland answered, "Our lady is yet to be fully dressed, I believe it will take another three weeks to have all in order. It takes time to set all standing rigging to exact tautness and exact alignments. We've stores to load, shot and power to be brought aboard and then there will be the need to add to the ship's company. So, having considered all these things, I dare to hazard a guess that we'll not receive orders for several weeks." He did not let on that all that he had just stated depended on whether or not Admiral Pigot would allow any of it.

"A few weeks then! I'll have just enough time to bed all the ladies a second time!" Sharpe stated with a huge grin.

What was said after that was lost in the haze of cigar smoke, backslapping and drinking. Poor Mister Mellencamp had not asked to be excused but as soon as the cigars were lit he became ashen and ran to the cabin door. David whispered something to Hornsby and left to seek out the boy. Donland had not missed the little drama and smiled, the custard was a bit too much for the lad.

Donland paced the deck. A full moon flooded the sea and the ship with light. Hornsby stood by the helm, it was his watch. He said nothing as Donland paced from stern to bow with his hands clasped behind his back. Seaman who shared the watch remained on the larboard side attending to their duties as their captain paced.

He paced out or restlessness and a full stomach. Other occasions had taught him to drink with diligence. A drunken captain was a poor example and a puking captain was one to be pitied.

Honest came on deck bearing a pitcher of water and a glass. "I thought you might have a bit of thirst."

Donland took the glass, "Aye, that was thoughtful of you. Simon asleep?"

Even in the moonlight Donland saw the smile.

"Aye, pots all scrubbed and put away. He'll not so much as turn over."

"A good lad," Donland said thoughtfully. "Once I'm confirmed," he said.

"Aye, I know," Honest answered. "And, he knows. He's studying hard and Mister Welles drills him with questions. He's as ready as any lad and I dare say in comparison to others of that station, he's more knowledgeable and equipped."

Donland replied, "Like Mister Welles, I believe one day he will walk his own deck."

"Aye," Honest said with pride. "He knows no other life and has no other dream. I just pray I will be there to see him get his step."

"Something on your mind?" Donland asked.

Honest sighed, "We've just finished with one war and already there's talk of another. That Captain Johnson, he told all he heard and thought and now all the lads are speculating. What do you think is in the offing?"

"Wars and rumors of war," Donland answered.

The answer did not please Honest, so he said, "Aye, that I know from the Bible but Captain Johnson was in the pub and going on and on about how we were heading for a war with France. Is it true?"

Donland did not hesitate, "There is always the rumor of war, you know that. We have seen uprisings where some fellow or another lusts for power over people and such a man will do whatever he can to gain it no matter the consequences. Perhaps war will come but if so, it will be the Frogs at war with one another. It'll not involve England unless the king is forced to flee. All the heads of Europe are bound by blood and you know the saying that blood is thicker than water. Royal blood is twice as thick for if one falls they are all in danger of falling. Should the king of France flee, then the heads of Europe will come against the usurper. That will be the time we should become concerned."

Honest nodded and said, "If the king flees then it will be on us."

"Aye, and if any of the gossips below deck get all in a lather, you be the prophet and proclaim there is no danger until the king flees."

Honest laughed, "Me be the prophet!"

"At least be the herald of good news."

Chapter Nine

Two days following *Oxford* hoisting her complete suit of sail the seventy gun *Prince Frederick* dropped her hook off Mosquito Point. The third lieutenant having sailed from English Harbor with just enough men to manage the sails delivered her to Commodore Pettibone.

Three hours later Powell came aboard *Oxford*. "She's to be a hulk for prisoners," he informed Donland.

He inquired, "And what of the Lieutenant?"

"Half-pay," Powell answered.

"Perhaps the commodore can be persuaded to pass him to me," Donland suggested.

"He's already signed the order and those aboard who wish to enter into *Oxford's* muster are given the choice. You may be interested to know that Admiral Pigot is to sail for England in a short while. Commodore Pettibone has decided he has need of *Oxford* and the stores, power and shot you have requested are to be sent across within a few days."

Donland wanted to shout for joy but he restrained himself and asked, "Will you be replacing Mister Halston?"

Powell half-smiled and said, "Once I've collected Lieutenant Rorie Malcolm and those willing to sign on."

"That," Donland said, "will please me greatly."

"There is another matter that I must make you abreast of, Commodore Pettibone must send notice to English Harbor that *Oxford* is ready for sea. He will only do that when news reaches him that Admiral Pigot and Warrior are returning to England."

Somewhat crest-fallen Donland said, "So I'm to endure more waiting, perhaps months more."

"Aye, but Pettibone told me to tell you, he'll not put it in writing, that once stores arrive, then *Oxford* needs to be put through her paces. He'll not certify her seaworthy until then."

"A free rein for a time will do me," Donland said with a wide grin.

"Aye, and will me!" Powell stated.

"But before we sail, I want to get some of the weed off her. If we can remove half, it will increase our speed considerably. I've little hope that the commodore, as helpful as he has been thus far, will stick his neck out to put her on the careening wharf."

"Have you a plan?" Powell asked.

Donland nodded and said, "We'll tow her near the beach, secure her to some large trees with tackles and blocks and wench her over as much as possible. I'll have the guns from larboard moved to starboard and have our men not on the capstan add their weight to larboard, should be enough to bring her over far enough to reach half the hull. Your thoughts?"

"I've not done such before but as I recall, you have on two occasions."

"Aye, but neither a frigate nor sloop have the tonnage of *Oxford*. It will be risky for if a wind or wave upset the balance she'll be dashed."

Powell mused, "The commodore would not care to have that on his report to Admiral Pigot. I would rather suggest the deed be done elsewhere. It will be more work on the company to remove stores, power shot and the like but away from prying eyes the better our chance of success."

Donland accepted Powell's reasoning. "I agree, then let us proceed with loading the stores. We've more than enough men for three watches of sail handling. My bones yearn to be at sea, I've enough of the land."

"As I," Powell said. He then ventured, "If Pigot sails before we return then the commodore should have no objections to our putting her over on the wharf."

"Aye, my mind was just coming to that as well, that would be all for the better."

The following week, with stores loaded and the addition of forty-two seamen and Lieutenant Malcolm, *Oxford* prepared to sail.

Everyone watched as Johnson's packet dropped her hook, none more so eager to meet with Johnson than Donland. What surprised him was a boat was put over and began making for *Oxford*. Donland pulled a glass from the rack and found the boat. To his amazement a lieutenant sat in the stern, it was not Johnson.

"Orders from Antigua?" Powell mused beside Donland.

"Perhaps, we can only hope. I will receive the lieutenant in my cabin, bring him if you please."

"Aye Captain," Powell answered.

The marine sentry opened the cabin door and in walked a familiar figure, grinning and with his hat in the crook of his arm. Behind him came a second familiar figure also grinning.

"Lieutenant Andrews as I live and breath," Donland said as he rose from his chair.

"Aye, Captain," Andrews answered while beaming.

Donland extended his hand and Andrews took it.

"Mister Aldridge, Sir," Andrews said as he shook Donland's hand.

Aldridge stepped forward, "It is so good to see you, Sir."

"And to see you," Donland said and again extended his hand.

"Have you orders?" Donland asked as he stepped back from the pair.

"We have not, sir. We've come with hopes and nothing more," Andrews explained and continued, "We heard you have your step and are fitting out *Oxford*. We hoped to join before others arrived."

"You know the regulations, post captains do not pick and choose. But, since you have arrived and I am indeed in need I will send my request straight away to Commodore Pettibone. There is but one berth remaining for a lieutenant and one remaining for a midshipman. I'll write the request this minute and you can carry it across to the commodore." Donland said and returned to his chair.

Andrews turned to Aldridge and slapped him on the back. "I told you he'd have us if we did not dawdle and some other step forward before us!"

Donland heard, "Aye, you reasoned it well Mister Andrews, I'd want no others. You and your ways are known to me just as mine are to you. You'd stood the test of fire more than once and both have proved your mettle. Someone once called his company, we happy few and said 'to glory we steer'. Let it be the same for our company."

"Aye, sir," Aldridge said in chorus with Andrews.

Donland sat alone in his cabin. The transom windows were thrown wide and a decent breeze blew into the fetid cabin. It was the middle of the first dog-watch and the temperature was as oppressive below deck as it was above. He sat without a shirt, the account books before him, charts littered the deck and the end of his table. The water in the glass at his elbow beckoned and he lifted it. Tepid, and unsatisfying.

Bending to his task he entered the date into the account book, May 18, 1784. Under the column headed *POWDER* he wrote two hundred. It occurred to him that *Hornet* had carried that amount and that *Oxford* was authorized almost three times the amount. He smiled, peace it may be but heaven help the captain forced into a fight with an inadequate supply of powder.

The sound of the stamp of boots followed by a tap at the door announced Powell's return.

Powell entered unbidden and made straight to the sideboard, he lifted the decanter of brandy and poured. "He'll not give us more men at the present!" Powell said and downed the brandy in a gulp.

"As I suspected," Donland said without anger or surprise. Then asked, "When are we to return?"

"Two weeks, ten days at the most."

"Ten days it will be," Donland said with a smile. He asked, "What of the master and pursuer?"

"Master is a fellow named Winslow, I've met him, near on forty I would say and from Kent. Experienced man to all accounts, he's sailed these waters for the better part of fourteen years. Pursuer is named Leeland, New York born, haven't met him. Both are to come over before nightfall. We're to have a surgeon, he'll also be coming aboard with the other two. His name is Linn. He's a Scott from Edinburgh."

Donland expressed his surprise, "Linn, the one who cured scurvy?"

"No, another but related. Considerably younger man, late twenties, a drinker and card player so I'm told."

"Returning to my initial question, are we to receive more men when we return?"

"Deuced if I know, Pettibone would not say yea or nay, only that he would consider adding to our company."

"Meaning that he is still waiting for Pigot's departure before completing fitting us out," Donland said and sighed.

"Aye," Powell said and picked up the Brandy bottle.

"You best not," Donland advised. "Two in this heat was not wise and a third will incur my anger for we've much to do."

Powell held the bottle for a moment, glanced at it and said, "Aye," as he replaced it on the sideboard.

Donland studied Powell for a moment and turned to stare out the window. The breeze had died. Powell's drinking was becoming a concern. He'd not voiced it as yet, but if the drinking did not abate, he would be forced to address it.

"I'll receive our new additions to the company at six bells after you've arranged their billets and evening meal. Mister Brunson, Mister Malcolm, Mister Andrews and Lieutenant Sharpe will attend us shortly afterwards for introductions."

"Aye, Captain," Powell replied well aware of Donland's displeasure.

The first to enter was the surgeon, Linn, a young man no more than twenty with bright curly red hair and full beard to match. He was thin with a fair complexion. Following him was an older man that Donland assumed to be the master, Winslow, he was squat with a rummy nose and balding brown hair. The pursuer, Leeland, was a shabby rotund man with graying muttonchops and a thick crop of gray hair. No doubt the man was well past forty.

Powell closed the door and began introductions. Donland was mindful of each man's formality and unease. He knew it would be that way and for that reason he chose to meet them as a group and then have them meet the others. Once under sail he would take time to interview each man separately but for now he wanted them to become familiar with his officers.

"Gentlemen thank you for coming to my cabin at this late hour. I'm certain you have much to do in preparation of our sailing tomorrow but I felt it needful that we become familiar with one another. Over the next ten days or so we will come to know each other better and to rely upon each other's experience, training and knowledge. Our voyage is to be short and for the purpose of sorting out. We have only a third of our company at present but upon our return we shall receive the remainder. In the meantime, let patience be manifest and in abundance." He paused and eyed them. "I've invited the ship's officers to join us and I believe them to be waiting. I will leave them to do their own introductions."

"Mister Powell would you invite your officers to attend?"

"Aye Captain," Powell said and opened the cabin door.

The lieutenants entered dressed in freshly laundered uniforms and shirts. Honest came in from the galley followed by Simon bearing trays of glasses filled with wine. Cheese and sweet meats were already on the table. The men began shaking hands and introducing each other. Some were already acquaintances and took the lead to make the other introductions. Donland stood off to the side and observed and only occasional indulged in short conversations.

Donland approached Powell who was standing amidships staring out past Mosquito Island to the open sea. A half-moon was just rising. From the shore, drifting on the evening breeze floated the sounds of drunken men at the nearby pub. There was music and the occasional harsh laugh of a woman.

"I'll be glad to be away from this for a few days," Donland said.

"Aye," Powell said as he turned to face his captain. "I was just thinking of how debauchery is like unto a fever, it begins down deep someplace and spreads until it consumes the body and mind. By such time little can be done to rein it in."

"Wine, women and song," Donland mused.

"Not good for a man used to the ways of the sea to linger too much among them," Powell added.

"Agreed," Donland said.

They were quiet for several moments. The seaman working the deck attended to tasks well away from the pair. Curious they may be but of respect, they keep their distance.

"I've put away the bottles," Powell confessed.

"Aye, I had no doubt you would," Donland said. "A good man knows the devil when he comes a calling. We've been friends, officers and fellow captains for a long time. I know you as well as I've ever known a man and I fear you know me equally. I've often considered how but for a decision made by others our roles could be reversed, you captain and me lieutenant. Have you?"

"That I have and I've tasted the bile of envy, swallowed it and accepted that good fortune has come my way often enough. So, I've no regrets. One day I will again stand on my own deck and as long as I share a deck with you I know the odds are in my favor. In fact, I was thinking earlier when Mister Andrews appeared on the wind, that there are those who seek you out. They know as I, that opportunity is always before you. Curious is it not?"

Donland laughed, he laughed from the gut. When the laughter subsided he said, "Fools see opportunities where wise men see folly. My curse is that duty robs me of good sense. What say you?"

"My good friend, let me assure you, your head is more stable than those adorned with powered wigs."

"That is not a great compliment, as you well know."

It was Powell's turn to laugh. "Aye, but I meant it to be one. I beg your forgiveness."

The bell clanged and Midshipman Mellencamp called in his boyish voice, "The glass is turned, Sir!"

The distraction allowed Donland to ask, "We were speaking of Mister Andrews, what value do you place on him?"

Powell gazed out to sea and answered, "As stout as oak, experienced and good with the men. He had a good captain at some point else he'd not be what he is."

"At least one," Donland mused. "I remember well my first encounter with him when I received command of *Hornet*. He was hatless, shirtless, unshaved, drunk and smelling of a whore. I gave him a choice and to this day I am pleased with his choice. He will one day walk his own deck, and to quote my old friend, Jackson, 'that's no err'."

"That is so, he has the head and the heart for command, as does Aldridge. I'm not surprised in the least that they have risked all on a whim and prayer to journey here in hopes of serving under you again."

Donland turned from the rail. He said, "Let us pray wisdom has not failed them." He smiled and said, "I shall go to my cabin, we will be required in a few hours and those hours will be better served in sleep."

"Aye," Powell agreed.

Chapter Ten

Donland stood firmly planted by the helm. He surveyed the deck in the faint light of pre-dawn. The tide would be on the wane in a matter of minutes, according to Winslow, the new master. All was in readiness, *Oxford* was his to command and the decision when to sail was his alone. She was neither a sloop, nor a frigate and to set her free was to be a new experience, one that he had not dreamed would come so soon in his career. He half-turned, caught sight of Winslow then turned toward Powell, "Very well, Mister Powell, get the ship under way, if you please."

Powell replied with a trace of excitement in his voice, "Aye, Captain!"

Turning back to Winslow, Donland said, "Lay a course to weather the point, deep water and put two strong mates on the wheel."

"Aye, Captain," Winslow answered.

Donland stepped to the rail and gazed down the deck at the length and breath of *Oxford*, his *Oxford*. Men were at their stations, the capstan was manned, Sharpe's marines stood by the mizzen braces. Bill and his mates were in the tops; their bare feet perched on the toe ropes.

Powell lifted the speaking trumpet he had acquired and put it to his mouth, "Ready the capstan!"

"Aye, sir!" Stewart the bo'sum called in reply.

Powell bellowed, "Loose the heads'ls! Hands aloft and loose tops'ls!"

The topmen, quick as cats, began to undo the lashings.

"Man the braces!" Powell shouted with gusto.

Men strained and groaned at the capstan bars and with great effort began pulling the massive anchor from the depths spilling a cloud of sand and silt as it rose.

With the aid of the receding tide and the push of wind *Oxford* tilted to the pressure. The sails, pulling taut, held the wind and *Oxford's* rudder challenged the pressure. Her deck responded by tilting more steeply and above the weather-hardened seamen responded to the challenges on the yards. They fought to control the bucking and kicking of the billowing folds of canvas.

"Hard over!" Winslow shouted and his two mates at the wheel shifted their weight and spun the great wheel.

Overhead came the creaking of yards as they bent like huge bows. With the sails hard and full, *Oxford* came alive as she gathered her way.

Donland half-smiled and thought, *she's no racehorse and certainly no frigate but she'll do me!*

The anchor was seized and catted by the hands, *Oxford* settled on her course as the sun broke the horizon. She crashed into the waves as it they were nothing more than a mild nuisance. The wind came from astern pushing her onward. Her bows began to lift and fall in rhythmical precision. The air above the deck was filled with the noise of whining rigging and the thud and bump of hard canvas. Bill and his mates working high above the deck appeared as large flying insects darting about from one sail to the next.

Powell was a creature of boundless energy let loose upon the deck. His trumpet was continually to his lips while pushing and smacking men to do his bidding. Brunson, likewise was as a mad-hatter. Only Lieutenants Malcolm and Andrews seemed at ease as they rushed from one task to the next.

Donland stood at the rail, his eyes missing nothing. From behind him Winslow said conversationally, "She's taking to it."

"Aye," Donland said without turning and added, "We'll let her have her head a little longer then I'll have a reef."

"Aye, Captain," Winslow acknowledged.

The bell clanged seven times. Men began to stream down from the tops for their dinner and their grog. Donland watched from the quarterdeck, he smiled, the morning had passed quickly and without incident. Wedges around each mast were tightened, stubborn blocks were taken down and replaced. A halyard forward had snapped, all typical for a morning. On the whole, the company preformed well. *Oxford*, however, was slow. Donland likened her to an old milk cow going out from the barn. By his estimation the weed on her bottom was slowing her by more than two knots.

"Beg pardon Captain, me dad says your dinner is ready," Simon said as he came beside Donland.

"Thank you, Simon, I'll come," he said to the boy.

Brunson had the watch, so he said to him, "South by southeast, Mister Brunson. Perhaps with the wind up our coattails it will shake loose some weed. You may take a reef if you deem it necessary but call me if the wind begins to veer."

"Aye, Captain," Brunson answered.

Honest stood beside the table waiting as Donland sat. He then lifted the lid on the platter to reveal a large filleted fish surrounded by small potatoes. "Simon caught it just this morning," Honest said as he poured water into a glass.

"Just the one?" Donland asked.

Honest smiled and said with pride, "He caught six, he's got the gift. One of the other lads got four and altogether they caught fourteen. I've a stew on for them."

Donland asked, "How many boys have we?"

"Eight younger than twelve. Their da's signed em' into the muster all proper."

"I've always tried to avoid having boys aboard, too much like having women."

Honest rubbed his chin and said, "Aye, I know. Devil's temptation that and them." He paused then said, "There be two that's slipped aboard."

Donland stared up at Honest and asked, "Two women?"

"Aye, came dressed as men, both married and both be mothers to lads."

"The bo'sum know?"

Honest nodded. "Aye, he told me, said he'd not seen them till this morning."

Donland chewed, swallowed and asked, "Did you believe him?"

Rather than answer, Honest sat and leaned in toward Donland. "He's crafty, sly as a fox. He'll bear watching."

The marine sentry at the cabin door shifted his weight and stamped his boot. Honest rose from the chair as a knock sounded.

"Enter!" Donland ordered.

David entered with his hat in the crook of his arm. "Beg pardon, Captain a sail has been sighted due south of us, two masts. Lieutenant Brunson requests your instructions."

"Observe only, set one of the mid-top men to keeping a watch."

"Aye, Sir," David answered and turned to go.

Donland waited until the door closed then said to Honest, "Have the two women brought to the office, I will interview them."

"You want their men?" Honest asked.

"I'll not," he answered. His appetite had left him, he picked up the water and drank. Setting down the empty glass he said, "Go fetch the women, I'll do it now as to not spoil another meal."

Honest followed the two women into the cabin and closed the door. Fear was etched into the two young women's faces. Both wore trousers, men's shirts and floppy hats. Donland estimated their ages to be early twenties.

"Remove your hats!" he barked.

Neither woman obeyed so Honest snatched their hats from their heads. Their eyes were wide with fear and they visibly shook.

Donland stared across his desk at them, he was in no mood to smile or be cordial. "You!" he said and pointed to the one who seemed to cower behind the other. "Where were you married?"

The woman did not answer.

"Answer the Captain or it will go bad for your man and boy," Honest said.

The woman turned and stared up into Honest's face then slowly faced Donland. In a whisper she managed "Kingston, in the little church."

"And you?" Donland asked the other woman.

With a tremble in her voice she said, "We've not, we've no money. Derry say we not need be married."

Donland folded his arms and leaned back studying the two women. He pointed to the one who claimed to be married, "What is the name of your son?"

"John," she said without hesitation.

"And yours?" he asked the other woman.

"Ah, er, his name be Matthew," she answered.

Donland stood and turned to face the window. He stood gazing out at the empty sea for more than a minute then turned to face the women. "Sentry!" he called.

The door instantly opened and the young marine entered with his musket raised.

"Escort these two women to the ward room and remain with them. Pass the word for Lieutenant Sharpe."

"Aye, Captain!" the marine answered.

Donland addressed the women, "Go with him and remain with him until I call for you. You'll not be harmed."

The women did as they were told and went ahead of the marine who still held his musket at the ready.

"I'll have the two boys," Donland said to Honest.

Surprise showed on Honest's face but he answered, "Aye, Captain," and went out.

Donland again seated himself behind his desk. A loud knock came before he was comfortable. "Enter!" he called.

Lieutenant Sharpe opened the door, removed his hat and saluted. "Captain may I be of service?"

"Aye, Mister Sharpe. There are two men aboard who have brought two women aboard. Take two of your men and collect those men, hold them until I send for them."

"Aye, Captain," Sharpe answered and turned sharply for the door.

Donland poured himself a glass of water. As he was drinking there came another knock at the door and Honest entered pushing two small boys ahead of him.

"These are the lads that came aboard with the women," he said to Donland. Then looking down to the boys he said, "This is Captain Donland, you answer truthfully or I'll have the hide off of you!"

The boys were wide-eyed, ragged and dirty.

"Which of you is named John?" Donland asked.

Neither boy spoke. Honest rapped his knuckles lightly against the shorter boy's head. "Speak up!" Honest said.

The boy was no more than eight and squeaked, "me."

Donland smiled at the boy, "What is your mam's name?"

The boy stood terrified and did not answer until Honest rapped him on the head. "Jane!" he managed.

"And your mam?" Donland asked the taller boy.

"Rosita," the boy answered instantly.

"That will be all, take them out," Donland ordered.

Honest appeared mystified but obeyed and led the two boys from the cabin.

Powell came through the door as Honest left. "Is this a matter I should concern myself with?" he asked.

"I think not, I've the matter in hand. You've the jest of it?"

"Aye, two men brought two women aboard. Whores?"

"I think not, but it matters not. I'll not have them aboard to cause disruptions. The men and their wives will be put off at the first opportunity and until such time they will be held under guard.

"Shall I attend to that?" Powell asked.

Donland considered the question and replied, "Lieutenant Sharpe may attend to it and assign his men to the task. I will leave it to you to inform him."

"Aye," Powell said and looked past Donland out the window. "You've not indicated a destination for this cruise."

Donland smiled, "I've not, I thought it best that we let her have her head and sort out the inadequacies before seeing how she responds to tacks. I'd not care to go about and lose the sticks."

"Aye, sensible, Sir."

A sharp rap at the door announced another visitor. "Enter!" Donland ordered.

Sharpe stepped into the cabin, made eye contact with Powell and saluted Donland. "The men are located and confined," he stated.

"Thank you, Mister Sharpe. I was just appraising Mister Powell of the situation. The men and their wives will be set ashore at our first opportunity. Until that time, it will be best if they are confined together. Mister Powell will find a suitable space."

"Aye, Captain doing so will lessen my task," Sharpe replied.

"Now gentlemen, if you please, see to the arrangements," Donland said and sat.

Honest tapped at the cabin door and entered. He asked, "Is there more to be done?"

Donland half-smiled. "No Honest there's not. I'm satisfied there was no mischief afoot to offer the women so I'll have the lot of them put ashore."

"You'll not keep the hands?"

Truthfully, Donland replied, "I did consider doing so but the tale will have gone throughout the company. Having done so those men will endure some ridicule and there will no doubt be remarks made to them and thus violence. Better to be done with it as soon as possible."

"Aye, sir, aye."

Donland changed tack, "You think the bo'sum was paid?"

Rather than answer, Honest laid a finger against his nose.

Donland nodded and said, "He'll bear watching."

Overhead came the clang of the bell.

"Muster, Sir," Honest acknowledged.

Donland began to rise and said, "Aye, we'll go up. I need the air."

Chapter Eleven

The ship's company assembled for the daily muster and each officer and petty officer took the accounting. Brunson, as officer of the watch, stood at the quarterdeck railing observing. Winslow's mate, an Irishman whispered to Brunson, "Captain!"

Brunson dutifully turned from the railing. "Captain, course is south by southwest."

"What of the earlier sail, Mister Brunson?"

"Merchantman, gave us a wide berth," Brunson answered.

"The muster, Mister Brunson?" Donland asked.

"All accounted for, one man below with the surgeon. Boils I believe, Sir."

Donland noted that Powell was conversing with Andrews by the mainmast. The conversation seemed heated. He deemed it time to give them something else to think about.

He turned to Winslow, "Mister Winslow she's had her way long enough, let us put her through her paces. What say you?"

Winslow grinned and replied, "Aye, Captain."

Donland checked the set of *Oxford's* sails and ordered, "Bring us onto a due west course then we shall tack due north."

"Aye, Captain, due west, then tack to due north!" Winslow replied.

Donland called, "Mister Powell we will sail due west! Be prepared to tack north!"

Andrews nodded to Powell, smiled and hurried to his station at the foremast.

Powell put his speaking trumpet to his lips and began shouting orders. Men in the tops responded quickly and efficiently. The marines were busily taking up the lines at the mizzenmast and Rorie Malcolm was moving among them.

Donland caught sight of the bo'sum, Stewart, cracking his starter against the backside of a slow moving seaman. The man turned and said something and the bo'sum leveled him with a punch.

"Due west!" Winslow called when *Oxford* came onto her course.

"Let her settle to it Mister Winslow!" Donland said without turning. His attention was on Powell who was facing off with the bo'sum.

"Heave!" Malcolm shouted to the marines.

Donland momentarily turned, the marines were having difficulty hauling tight the mizzen. It cleared and the sail became taut.

As Donland turned, he glimpsed Brunson pushing a seaman to where he wanted him. By that time, the drama between the bo'sum and Powell had ended.

Oxford settled on her due west course. It was apparent enough to Donland that the company was made up of experienced men, but they had yet to work together as a company. It would remain for the lieutenants to drill their divisions into performing their tasks without thought.

"Mister Mellencamp, a glass from the rack if you please," Donland called.

The boy was quick off the mark and handed Donland a glass.

There was nothing to see but the distraction would serve the purpose. He wanted them ready for his command. A few moments of pause would not go amiss. He shut the glass and handed back to the midshipman.

"Mister Winslow, due north if you please," Donland said.

"Aye, Captain!"

"Helm! Hard over larboard!" Winslow called to the helmsman

Donland shouted. "Tack, due north!"

Powell lifted his trumpet, "Mains'l haul!"

The men responded for they were ready for the order when it came, as were the men of the other divisions. Donland watched as bowlines and braces were cast off and the yards came ponderously round. The foremast was slower than the main but they corrected and managed.

"Meet her!" Winslow snapped to the helmsman.

Oxford responded sluggishly and Donland was thankful he was not facing an enemy. The rudder seemed to act as a brake or perhaps, Donland thought, it's the weed. Overhead a line parted with a crack. He glanced up.

Powell's voice came above the din of flapping sail and jangle of blocks and cordage, "Haul off all!"

Seconds dragged by, the mizzen sails sagged then were brought taut by the struggling marines.

"Hold her, you there lend a hand!" Winslow was shouting with frustration.

Donland glanced down at the boxed compass, a point off due north. "One point larboard!" he shouted.

The red-faced Winslow replied, "Aye, Captain!" and thumped a young helmsman on the ear.

Oxford settled to her new course at half her previous pace. Her deck pitched and rolled as the waves struck her from amidships.

"We've not enough ballast," Winslow remarked.

"Aye, without stores, shot, power and a full company she's a drunken sailor on cobblestones," Donland said and grinned. He loosened his grip on the railing, turned and stared aft. *Oxford's* wake disappeared into the waves. "I fancy a stroll forward, hold her on this bearing until I return."

"Aye, Captain," Winslow acknowledged.

The men working the deck moved quickly from Donland's path. Those unencumbered saluted and those whose hands were occupied with tasks nodded.

"Mister Powell have you water?" Donland asked as he neared Powell.

"Aye, Captain, just yonder he said and pointed to a bucket," Powell answered.

Just then one of the boys rushed past carrying another bucket of water. The lad removed the near empty bucket and replaced it with the full one.

The boy seemed not to notice his captain and hurried away.

Donland watched the boy go then turned back to Powell. "Our people handled the tack in decent fashion did they not?"

"Aye, sir, a bit slow but with no more men available than we have, I'm pleased."

"As I," Donland said then added, "We will go about when I return to the quarterdeck. We've no Frog giving chase so we've no need to rush it."

"That is so, but standards have to be maintained. Don't you agree?"

"Aye, I do. When we've a full company, I'll brook no poor sail-handling. You would not."

"That is true, Captain. Old and slow *Oxford* might be but there are standards.

"Aye," Donland answered. He took two steps then turned about and asked, "The rigging, anything amiss or any complaints?"

Powell glanced up then back at Donland, "There are adjustments to be made, I'll have them in hand by the time you return to the quarterdeck."

Donland merely nodded, turned then continued on to the foremast where Andrews waited. "How is it with you?" he asked.

"Mast needs a good soaking and the wedges driven tighter," Andrews answered.

"You be the judge, furl the sails and drive the wedges while we are on this heading. My intention is to go about after I've done my inspection."

"Aye, Captain, I should be ready," Andrews said.

Andrews craned his neck and shouted up to the foremast division, "Brail up!" To those on the deck he commanded, "Haul taut and stop in the riggings!"

Donland walked on to the bow as Andrews continued shouting a stream of orders. He let his mind briefly drift to a time that he was in command of a foremast division. The smile was brief but did not go unnoticed by a man lounging on the sprit bow.

"You seem pleased to be at sea," the bare-footed bearded man wearing a floppy hat said.

Donland studied the man and wondered who he was to remain sitting on the sprit bow while casually conversing with his captain.

"Beg pardon Captain Donland," the man said as he slid to his feet and removed the hat. "It's my favorite place when I'm aboard ship."

"Doctor Linn!" Donland managed.

"Yes, it is I. My presence and appearance were not expected and I fully understand your failure to recognize me. Clothes do not the man make, so I've heard."

Donland managed a half-smile. He wanted to ask why the surgeon was not dressed according to his station but refrained. He did ask, "Doctor are you more comfortable afloat than on land?"

"Oh no, Captain, I prefer solid ground under my feet but as I'm obligated to the navy, I see no reason that I should not enjoy the best it has to offer. Hence, my perch and my shoeless-ness. I'm sure you have noticed that those of your command without shoes appear healthier than those with shoes or, as in your case, boots."

Donland could not help but look down at his boots and be reminded of his encased bone white feet. "Perhaps," he said.

Linn smiled broadly and suggested, "A little sun for your feet would aid your overall health."

Again Donland managed, "Perhaps." He turned his attention to the open sea before *Oxford* and was considering returning to the bridge. Linn's next words stopped him.

"You seem to enjoy that word, Captain. No doubt by the time this voyage has concluded our conversations will take on more substance. I should like that for I detect that there is a good deal more to you. We've a mutual acquaintance who speaks highly of you, your bravery and resourcefulness. He in fact urged me that if ever I have opportunity to sail with you that I should do so."

"An acquaintance?" Donland asked.

"Mathias," Linn said.

"Mathias Sumerford of Boston and Charleston?"

"There is only the one, he asked me to remember him to you. And, I must confess I cannot abide his filthy habit, I do not allow him to smoke them in my presence."

Donland knew instantly that Linn was more than an acquaintance of Sumerford's. Mathias' fondness of black tarry cheroots was as Linn said, annoying. "A man of secrets," Donland said and smiled.

"That he is and as you, I've shared a few with him. Anyway, Captain Donland, he is a shared acquaintance that will allow us to have some interesting conversation over brandy. I trust you've a bottle?"

"I do and perhaps you'll dine with me this evening?"

"Thank you, Captain for your gracious invitation. I shall be delighted to dine."

Donland nodded and said, "My coxs'un is a decent enough cook, rough fare mind you. Unless hindered, dinner is at eight."

"I shall look forward to the meal and the conversation," Linn said.

Returning to the quarterdeck, Donland put *Oxford* through her paces. They went about, tacked and went about again. It was hot tiring work for all aboard exhausting officers and seamen alike. As the sun dipped below the horizon, they were again sailing southwest under light sail.

"I've not been in these waters in ten years," Donland said to Winslow as they watched the sun disappear.

"We should sight Isla San Pio after daybreak if we remain on this heading. Might do well to bear off five points," Winslow suggested.

"No we will remain as we are, we'll lie-to for the night. Our company has done well today and a night of rest is well earned," Donland answered.

"Aye, and what of tomorrow?"

"More sail drill, and I think I should like to cruise the coast of Panama. I'd like to see how she will respond to squalls."

"Squalls, aye, there will be more'n enough if we run towards Colon. It's the season," Winslow replied.

They were silent a few moments. Winslow broke the silence by saying, "Almost lost my life a few years ago along the coast, fool captain wanted to take a prize, Spaniard he believed was carrying gold to Spain."

"A rich prize was it?" Donland asked.

"Fool captain didn't heed my warning and ran her aground, ripped the bottom, and all but sunk."

"No gold?"

"No gold!" Winslow said and turned to the helm.

Donland did not miss the man's disappointment.

Honest mused from behind Donland, "I think he wanted that gold as bad as his captain."

"As bad as you?" Donland asked.

"I'd not turn down a share," Honest answered.

Donland changed to a practical matter, "Doctor Linn will dine with me tonight. He said he is a friend of Sumerford."

"I've a fresh rat to stew," Honest joked.

"Have we ham?"

"Aye, that with potatoes and sliced fried papaya on the side should do you and him."

"I'll not complain," Donland responded.

Oxford rolled gently on the sea. All sail was furled, no one was in the tops and most of the ship's company lounged about on the main deck. There were card and dice games, a fiddle played along with two flutes. Andrews and Hornsby had the watch and remained on the quarterdeck passing the time in conversation. The helmsman, Johnson, and the master's mate a man named French ignored each other. Below deck, Donland and Linn were drinking brandy after having finished off their dinner. Honest and Simon were clearing away the dishes. The transom windows were flung wide.

Linn was the first to broach the subject of Sumerford. "Mathias works to his own ends, others be damned. Have you not found this to be true?"

Donland sipped his brandy and considered Linn's question. He answered, "He saved my life, has he told you of it?"

"No, he'd not spoken of it. I would assume it was in connection with some scheme or the other, one that would benefit either himself or his investors."

"Those things I have no knowledge of for as you have said, he keeps his cards close to his vest. I can tell you that we've sailed together on numerous occasions, faced storm and enemies side by side. There were times that he was under my orders and at others I under his. Even so, through it all we managed to develop friendship."

"I take it then that you trust him?" Linn inquired.

Donland drank from his glass and sat it down. He leaned in toward Linn, for some reason the question rankled. "When a man has saved your life and you his, there is a bond that goes beyond the word trust. I may not support some things he does or is engaged in but I would trust him and willingly stand by his side. And, I would not care to hear anyone disparage him."

Linn understood perfectly what Donland was saying to him. The words, though not direct, erected a boundary he best not cross. "He's working for the Americans now, are you aware of his involvement with them?"

Donland realized his caution was justified, Linn was skilled at probing with words and he wondered if the man was equally skilled with a knife.

"Yes, he purchased my ship for them and having done so, knowing him as I do, that the relationship with them goes deeper. But, he is not, nor will ever be the king's enemy. So, you may probe as you wish but I'll not say a word against him." His words gave rise to anger and he concluded, "I would hazard to assume that your presence aboard my ship was contrived by others. Is that so?"

"It was," Linn said

Donland was surprised by Linn's frankness and saw it as just another tactic to induce him to slander Sumerford. He cared not for the cat and mouse so he said, "You are a supernumerary aboard this ship, I command and you are under my orders as long as you are aboard. Since you are aboard under the direction of others, I feel I must make clear to you that I find trickery and the like offensive. If you are sent to gain information about me and my associations, then sir, ask your questions with honesty and integrity and I shall answer in like fashion."

Linn picked up his glass and sipped the brandy. He stood and moved to the sideboard, lifted the decanter and refilled his glass. "Another drop for you?" he asked Donland.

"I've sufficient," Donland answered as he stood.

"To clear the matter between us, I've not been ordered to spy on you or to inquire about Mister Sumerford. Rather, I ask my questions for myself. I have known Mathias since I was a lad. In these latter years, we've engaged in various enterprises together. Some were to our profit, and some to the profit of the king. As they say, in for a penny, in for a pound. Our association and friendship, perhaps lacking the same bond as yours, is something I dearly value. I would, therefore, like to forge a similar one with you. I view this conversation as a beginning."

Donland said nothing. He wanted to laugh at what he considered the absurdity of the conversation. He gazed out the windows to the blackness of the sea. There was no moon and very few specks of glowing light in *Oxford's* wake.

"As you say a beginning, let us drink a toast to Mathias and move on to other topics," Donland said and lifted his glass.

"To friendships, now and to come," Linn proposed.

The crack of musket fire reverberated from the jungle-encased shoreline. Lieutenant Sharpe requested that his marines be allowed ashore with the watering party. "Do my lads good to go ashore and practice their marksmanship."

Donland stood on the quarterdeck with his hands behind his back. Men were busy with the holystones, others with tar and grease were aloft and two miscreants were polishing the bell and other brass.

"Will you be going ashore?" Powell asked.

"No Mister Powell, I'm content to stand on this quarterdeck. Are you not equally content to be aboard?"

"Aye, Captain, I feared I'd not the opportunity again just as all these have also harbored such fears. Strange isn't it that having cursed a thing a man can love it?"

"The line is thin between hate and love," Donland said. He made a similar statement to Linn before Linn had departed after dinner. He still was not sure in his mind that he trusted the man. There had remained an evasiveness to the man. It was perhaps his nature and he'd known similar men.

"Boat pulling off, Captain!" Midshipman Welles called.

Donland turned, saw the boat loaded with men and barrels and nodded. Even at the distance to the land he thought he felt the afternoon heat of the jungle. The thought reminded him of Puerto Rico, how the heat sapped his strength. In his mind's eye he saw *Brune* exploding. He put the thought of the event away.

"We will sail as soon as the marines are aboard. Send the recall if you please Mister Welles."

"Aye, Captain," Welles answered.

"What of the wind, Mister Winslow?" Donland asked.

Winslow pursed his lips and replied, "Be the same for an hour or more. I suggest we bear off nor'west then tack more easterly for Colon."

"Aye, as I had in mind," Donland agreed.

"Beg pardon Captain," Brunson said approaching Donland. "Derry has asked if you intend to set his family ashore here."

"I am not that heartless Mister Brunson, he and the others will be sent ashore at Colon where they may find employment. He is owed a few pennies and will be paid."

"Aye, Sir, I will tell him," Brunson said and turned away.

"Lieutenant Sharpe has acknowledged, Sir," Welles said.

"Thank you, Mister Welles," Donland replied and said to Powell, "Prepare to get underway once the boat is stowed. I will be in my cabin."

"Aye, Captain," Powell responded.

Donland busied himself with logs and ledgers while the boats were hoisted in and the ship got underway. He was just finishing when he heard a loud thump on the deck overhead and a string of curses from Winslow. It was not a matter for him to deal with and he smiled to himself as he closed his personal log.

Honest set a plate in front of him, it was a small cake. He set beside the plate a goblet containing a yellowish liquid.

"What is this?" Donland asked.

Honest smiled, "Rosita, one of the women prepared this for you. She made two for she knew I'd not serve you unless I first ate it. Bit too sweet for my taste. The juice is pineapple. One of the lads on the water party is a Spaniard; he said he ate them when he was little more than a bairn. Rosita saw them and begged him for two. One she sliced and gave her son and the other she squeezed into a cup for you. It's a bit like lemon with lots of sugar."

The cake appeared to be coated with honey and nuts. He picked it up, examined it and took a small bite. It was sweet and nutty on the outside and the inside was a delicate sweet cake. "Delicious," he exclaimed. "I've never had the like."

He lifted the goblet and sipped the juice. It was sweet and thick, unlike anything he had before. The nearest taste that came to mind was the sweet apple cider his father had given him when he was a little boy.

After he finished, he said, "Tell Rosita it was wonderful and thank her for sending it to me."

"Aye, sir, I'll tell her," Honest said.

A low rumble came to Donland's ear. At first he thought he imagined it but the look on Honest's face reassured him he had not. "Guns," he said.

"Aye, some distance," Honest agreed.

"Let us see what is afoot," Donland said and reached for his hat. Honest fetched the coat from where it was hung.

Chapter Twelve

David stood at the door about to request entry when Donland opened the door. "Mister Powell's compliments, Captain, he reports hearing gunfire."

"Aye," Donland said.

"Where away, Mister Powell," Donland asked.

"I believe two shots to the southeast of us. There's no sail sighted so I've sent Bill to the top of the mainmast."

Donland craned his neck while holding his hat on and spied Bill nearing the topmost yard. Still the small man climbed until hands grasped the cap.

"Gawd that man can climb and has no fear!" David remarked in amazement.

Donland strained to hear what Bill was saying but couldn't make it out. What he did understand was the direction Bill pointed.

"Alter course five points larboard if you please, Mister Winslow, we shall investigate," Donland said.

"Shall we beat to quarters?" Powell asked.

Donland considered for a moment and said, "I think not, we'll show our colors and approach. Send up another man to relay what Bill sees."

"Aye, Captain," Powell answered and called to Malcolm, "Mister Malcolm, take a glass and go up!"

"Aye, Sir!" the young lieutenant responded and hurried to the quarterdeck for the glass.

Winslow said, "Any more than five points and we'll be close hauled."

"Aye," Donland agreed and added, "I'll order a tack if needed."

"Mister Powell, call all hands if you please."

"Aye Captain," Powell said and lifted his speaking trumpet.

Malcolm snatched a glass from the rack and began to climb the shrouds. The wiry youth reminded Donland of the times as a young man that he had done so. *Reckless abandonment*, he thought.

Sharpe's marines trooped up a hatchway and quickly assembled into two ranks. Sergeant Hawkes booming voice carried above the noise of other men rushing to their stations, the wind and the creaks of rigging and masts. Had Powell his voice he'd not need the trumpet.

Malcom called down, "Three sail! Close inshore!"

"Can you see them Mister Malcolm?" Donland shouted.

"Not yet, Sir!"

"Mister Winslow, ten points to larboard, if you please," Donland ordered.

"Aye, Captain," Winslow said and repeated to the helmsman, ten points larboard.

Powell lifted his trumpet and called, "All hands! Trim sail!"

The deck was alive as men hauled on lines to bring the sails into alignment with the wind and the heading of the ship. There was instantly a marked decrease in speed.

"We'll not gain but a knot on them," Donland remarked.

"At least we will see what they are about," Powell said as the roll of two more cannon shot reached *Oxford*.

"Aye, that is my intention Mister Powell. Best that we are out of danger but close enough to observe."

"Pirates do you imagine?" Winslow asked.

"Most likely, Mister Winslow, most likely," Donland mused. He added, "I make it about three hours of light remaining."

"Aye, and little moon tonight. They'll have to lie-to in the dark as near in to the coast as they are."

An hour passed before *Oxford* drew near enough to the three ships that Malcolm was able to call down, "Spanish flags!"

Donland studied the set of *Oxford's* sails. He considered the strength and direction of the wind. "Mister Winslow what is your opinion of the wind?"

"Veering two points from nor'west, it will hold that till after dark then die."

"Perhaps we can make up some distance."

Donland turned to Powell, "Stun'ls Mister Powell."

"Aye, Captain," Powell replied and grinned.

Powell lifted his speaking trumpet and ordered, "Rig stun'ls!"

"Lively there, Mister Andrews!"

Andrews called, "Square the yards! Braces and yard-tackles!"

Donland observed as the stun'ls were prepared to be hauled aloft. He was somewhat surprised at the speed the men were accomplishing the task having only been drilled in it once.

Oxford's speed immediately increased with the addition of the stun'ls even though a slight change in helm had cost them thrust.

"I do believe we're gaining," Winslow remarked.

Throughout the maneuver the rumble of cannon shot still reverberated. Donland wondered if any assistance they might lend would come too late.

"I shall go up," he said and took a glass from the rack.

He was not as swift a climber as the young Malcolm but he was determined not to embarrass himself. Reaching the mainmast fighting top, he put the glass to his eye. The larger vessel, a two-decker, perhaps a cut-down third-rate or a large frigate, was being pursued by two sloops. All three bore Spanish ensigns. It was a queer circumstance.

One of the sloops was attempting to far-reach the larger vessel while the other trailed astern of her firing a bow-chaser. The distance between the trailing sloop and the two-decker was such that hits were unavoidable. It was only a matter of time before the two-decker was forced to turn and fight or surrender.

Donland reached a decision and called down, "Mister Powell gather a gun crew for the forward starboard thirty-two!"

"Aye, Captain!" Powell called up.

Donland observed the chase for a few minutes longer. The two-decker was not without her teeth and appeared to have leveraged one of her heavy guns to her transom and fired a blast of grape or chain at her pursuer. The distance was still too great to measure the damage but he was certain the blast had hit home. "That should give me some time," he said to himself.

Gaining the deck, he was met by Powell who stated, "We are well out of range."

"Aye," Donland agreed. "However, all three captains will know our intention is to close and sort out the matter. They'll not know we haven't the gun crews aboard but when they see all the ports open at once we'll have put the fear of God in them, so we will!"

Powell's face registered delight at the idea. "Aye, that it will!" He managed.

"I should think Mister Andrews is best suited to command the gun," Donland said.

"Aye, he is quite the marksman with a long nine but he has yet to be proven with the thirty-two. Perhaps we should load three guns, may as well give the lads practice," Powell suggested.

"I considered doing such, one shot may not be sufficient to cause them to break off the action. We've little time before darkness overtakes us and I want to close as near as prudent while we can see."

"Three guns then?" Powell asked.

"Aye, make it so if you please Mister Powell."

It took all of ten minutes to load and train the three large cannons. *Oxford* had closed within two miles of the three ships and there was yet an hour of daylight remaining.

Powell reported all three guns loaded and a man was stationed at each gun port on the starboard side. When the shot was fired, it was to signal the opening of all ports.

"The starboard gun is laid and the port is open. Mister Andrews assures me that the shot will fall close enough to be observed by their lookouts. Surely, they have seen us."

"Aye, they have and they know we intend to interfere. Have Mister Andrews fire gun one."

"Aye," Powell said and lifted his speaking trumpet. "Fire gun one!" He shouted.

Brunson relayed the order and the big gun boomed belching fire and smoke.

Firing at maximum elevation it was nearly impossible to see the fall of shot from the quarterdeck. Donland trained his glass on the trailing sloop but could see no discernable reaction. He did feel the slight rumble of all the ports springing open. Still, he saw no reaction.

"Mister Welles take this glass and go into the shrouds. When the next shot is fired, attempt to see where it lands," Donland said and handed the glass to David.

"Aye, Captain," David answered and took the glass.

Donland waited until David was situated and ready to observe the shot.

"The second gun, if you please Mister Powell," Donland ordered.

Again, Powell lifted the speaking trumpet and ordered, "Mister Andrews, fire gun two!"

The order was repeated by Brunson and the gun boomed.

As the smoke drifted away, David called, "A chain short of the aft quarter of the two-decker!"

"That will give them concern!" Powell said with glee.

"Aye," Donland replied.

"What is the rear sloop about Mister Welles," Donland called.

David focused on the glass onto the sloop and studied it for a couple of minutes. Donland was growing impatient but said nothing. David lowered the glass and turned to face him, "She's altering course, Captain!"

"Mister Mellencamp, advise Mister Andrews to target the rear sloop!" Donland commanded the young midshipman.

"Aye, Captain," The boy answered and set off at a run.

"Walk, Mister Mellencamp!" Powell ordered the boy.

Mellencamp immediately slowed and then jogged to the hatch and disappeared down to the gun-deck.

Donland waited nervously for Andrews to acknowledge the order and respond that he was ready.

Brunson called, "Gun ready, Sir!"

"Fire gun three if you please, Mister Powell," Donland ordered.

The order was relayed and the gun boomed.

David was watching for the fall of shot, he called, "Hit her!"

"Shot punched her sails!"

Donland was amazed.

Those on deck broke into a cheer, "Huzza! Huzza! Huzza!"

"Gun one ready!" Brunson called.

Oxford was still closing slowly on the trio of ships, but closing nonetheless.

"Lead sloop is breaking away, changing course!" David called. A few seconds later he called, "Rear sloop is falling astern!"

"That's done for them then!" Powell said with a hint of excitement.

"Aye, take in the stun'ls Mister Powell."

"Aye, Captain," Powell responded.

"Two-decker is coming up on the wind!" David called.

"He's to render his thanks," Winslow said.

"Perhaps," Donland mused.

From behind him Doctor Linn said, "There is that word again, perhaps."

Donland turned to see the doctor grinning. He said to him, "Perhaps there are wounded men aboard that Spanish ship. If they are need of medical attention, you will be going across to them. You best go below and prepare your equipment."

"Mister Sharpe," Donland called. "Send your men below but have them at the ready. At the first hint of treachery I shall call for you."

"Aye, Captain," Sharpe responded and began issuing orders.

The stun'ls were being stowed and *Oxford* was still carrying her full suit of sails. "Mister Powell, pass the word to Mister Andrews, I'll have those three guns loaded. Close all other ports but those three are to remain open!"

"Aye, Captain," Powell answered. "What of our sail?"

"Two reefs each, we will maintain our way."

"Mister Winslow, I'll have two men on the wheel, if you please," Donland ordered.

Winslow was not surprised and answered, "Aye, Captain."

"Beg pardon, Captain, the Spaniard is signaling," David said.

The flags that were hoisted above the two-decker were from the English naval code book. Donland read them, *require assistance, enemy in sight.*

"They have our book," Powell said.

"Aye, and I have one of theirs," Donland replied with a half-grin. He did not add that the Spanish signals book was three years old.

The gap between the two ships closed steadily, the sun was well down below the horizon.

"Reef all sails, if you please Mister Powell, we will lie-to," Donland ordered as his mind considered possibilities.

In the twilight, the Spaniard lowered a boat. Someone in the boat lit a lantern.

"We shall have guests, a lantern, if you please Mister Welles. Take it down the side and wait for their boat to tie on," Donland ordered.

"Aye, Captain," David answered and removed a lantern kept by the compass box.

"Mister Powell, pass the word there are to be no lights aboard!"

"Aye," Powell called then tasked Aldridge to go deck by deck to make sure there were no lit lanterns.

The Spaniard's boat bumped alongside. Donland left the quarterdeck and made his way to the sally port. He arrived as David came up carrying the lantern. He was followed by a Spanish lieutenant. The others remained in the boat.

"I am lieutenant Don Louis Hernadez of his royal majesty's *Galicia*. Who do I have the honor of addressing?"

Donland answered, "I am Captain Isaac Donland, I welcome you."

"Ah, Captain Donland, late of the sloop *Hornet*, it so good to meet you at last. You have often been a thorn in my Captain's side. His name is Juan Francisco de la Bodega y Quadra. Before *Galicia* he commanded the magnificent *Princesa Real* which gave chase when you escaped Puerto Rico. Were it not for contrary winds we would have caught you."

"Perhaps, but that was another day, how may I and my ship be of assistance to you and your captain?"

"My Captain sends me to express his gratitude for your assistance in driving away the pesky pirates. They were as a pack of hyenas nipping at the lion's tail."

"May I offer you refreshment below?" Donland asked.

"Thank you but no, my captain desires I return once having expressed his appreciation."

"I've a surgeon aboard; perhaps you have wounded requiring attention?"

Hernandez quickly responded, "Alas no, all are well, nothing more than scratches and a few bumps. We've our own doctor. The pirates are very bad shots unlike your gunners."

"Yes I do have expert artillerymen aboard, they enjoyed the additional practice," Donland said tongue-in-cheek.

"Again, it has been a pleasure to meet you and again please accept my captain's gratitude for your intervention. Now, I must return before I become lost in the dark."

"Lieutenant Hernandez will *Galicia* lie-to for the night?" Donland inquired.

"Captain Quadra has not informed me of his intentions as yet," Henandez said as he made to exit.

Powell heard what was said and once Hernandez was away asked, "Shall I double the watch?"

"Aye, double the watch and have Lieutenant Sharpe add four of his marines for each watch. The Spaniard will not be showing any lights and we shall likewise remain dark."

"You don't trust him?"

"There is much not to trust, all three ships flew the flag of Spain. And, I suspect the *Galicia* is carrying valuable cargo. Then there is the matter of the code book and Hernandez's reluctance to accept the surgeon aboard his ship."

Powell said, "Do you think *Galicia* was taken and the sloops were attempting to retake her?"

Donland almost said, perhaps, but caught himself and said instead, "It is possible, and it is possible that we are in danger. Arm those of the watch and remind them to be vigilant. It is best that they investigate and report any sound no matter how insignificant. We have a former enemy within hailing distance lying-to that is not to be trusted. And let us not forget the two sloops. Anyone or all of the three could be flying false flags."

"Aye, it is a kettle of fish and we've no hooks," Powell said.

"You understand our danger," Donland said.

Chapter Thirteen

The night was lightly lit by the sliver of moon. *Oxford* rolled on a quiet sea and less than a cannon shot away the faint shape of *Galicia* sat like a ghost. Donland slept fitfully and every other hour he rose and to stand on the quarterdeck staring out at the ghost. Each time he encountered Powell who was equally sleepless. They spoke few words and when false dawn began to light the sea, they were side by side.

"Mister Powell, we shall make sail before our Spanish friend. Call all hands," Donland said. In one of their previous meetings in the night it was agreed to err on the side of safety and be underway before the Spaniard.

The twitter of the bo'sum's pipe broke the tranquilly of the pre-dawn. The sound of bare feet slapping on the deck and the hoots and cajoling associated with a ship getting underway completed shattering the stillness.

"Let us make good use of the wind we have Mister Winslow, set our course west by nor'west," Donland said as Winslow gained the deck.

"Aye, Captain," Winslow answered.

"She's letting down her sails," Powell observed.

"Aye, he's not slept either. Send a man up to the crosstrees to seek out those sloops, they'll not be far. I think they may be showing a light." Donland said with certainty.

"They may have given up now that they know they are over matched," Powell surmised after sending Watson to the crosstrees.

"True, but we best assume both are still about," Donland said as he studied *Galicia*. She was attempting to sail close-hauled on toward Colon.

"You're not going to pursue her?" Powell asked.

"Not as yet, if she is out of danger then we have no interest. Our task is to complete this cruise and return to Port Royal. You know as I, that there are those who will find fault with our interference. And, should we be damaged it could go badly, it is a risk I have to weight."

"Aye," Powell replied. "It is peace and we've no obligation."

The distance between *Oxford* and *Galicia* began to grow. The sky was beginning to brighten as the sun approached the horizon. Donland waited patiently.

"Deck there! Two sloops!" Watson called down to the deck.

"Where away?" Powell called up to Watson.

"East! Off the larboard quarter! Ahead of the Don!"

"We'll go about Mister Powell, let us sort it!"

"You've weighted it then?" Powell asked with a grin.

"If you please, Mister Powell!" Donland said with irritation.

"Aye, Captain," Powell answered and put the speaking trumpet to his lips. "All hands! Prepare to tack larboard! We will go about!"

Oxford had just enough way on her to manage the maneuver. As the sails swung round, Donland brought a glass to his eye and focused on *Galicia's* deck. He had difficulty making out the officers on her quarterdeck but not the flurry of activity as the crew prepared the guns on her upper deck.

"They intend to fight," Donland said to those standing near.

Powell was still bellowing orders as *Oxford* continued her turn. *Galicia* was also tacking true north to cross the wind and gain more distance from the sloops. It would be a slow maneuver and one the sloops could easily counter. They would have her in gun range before *Oxford* could bring a gun to bear. Captain Quadra would be hard pressed to fight off the sloops and keep them from boarding. His only hope would be to give up attempting to outsail the sloops and to go about to come under the protection of *Oxford's* guns.

Oxford continued her turn, sails flapped, Malcolm cussed and cajoled those of the mizzen to haul and move their arses. Forward, Bunson and Andrews likewise pushed, shoved and cursed their men to be quicker.

Oxford was all but in irons!

"Mains'l haul!" Powell bellowed at the top of his lungs forgetting the speaking trumpet.

"Cast off bowlines and braces!"

"Haul! Haul!"

Winslow shouted to the helmsman, "Now! Hard over!"

The rudder was biting but with *Oxford* quickly loosing her way, it was having little effect.

Andrews had the foremast sails in position, the sails were filling.

"Haul off all!" Powell shouted to Brunson who was having difficulty getting enough men from one position to the next. He simply did not have enough hands.

In frustration, Powell starting pushing men and gave the occasional kick.

"Haul you bastards!" Powell shouted and they did.

Oxford's mainsails filled and she began to move ever so slowly forward.

"East by nor'east!" the helmsman called.

"Two points more!" Winslow shouted to the helmsman as he studied the compass and gauged the wind.

The faint roar of cannons drifted on the wind. Donland held the glass to his eye studying the two sloops and did not miss their firing. Turning the glass to *Galicia*, he was certain her rigging was the target. The sloops meant to dismast her not sink her.

"Mister Powell, I will have the three forward starboard guns loaded and run out, if you please! Set Mister Andrews to it! Send Mister Aldridge to assist! Mister Hornsby can manage the forecastle!"

"Aye, Captain," Powell answered.

"They are trying to take her before we can assist," Winslow observed.

"Aye, Mister Winslow they mean to board her and carry off whatever it is they are seeking."

"Gold do you think Captain Donland?" Winslow asked.

"We shall see, Mister Winslow, we shall see."

Oxford was parallel but still more than a mile distant to *Galicia* and the sloops. Close enough to fire but not close enough to be accurate. *Oxford* was gaining in speed, Donland decided to close the gap. "Take us as close to the wind as she'll sail Mister Winslow."

He called to Powell, "Close hauled and close to the wind Mister Powell! I mean to close with her!"

"Aye Captain, Powell answered.

Donland lifted the glass to his eye and focused. There was some damage to *Galicia's* sails and rigging but she was making her turn, she'd have enough wind to half the distance between them in a matter of minutes.

Hornsby shouted from the foremast, "Mister Andrews reports guns are loaded and run out!"

Brunson relayed the message.

"Target the sloops!" Donland ordered.

"Aye, Captain, target the sloops!" Brunson replied and relayed the message down to the gun deck.

Oxford seemed to be creeping along, the weed on her bottom acting as a sea anchor. If and when they reached Port Royal, Donland promised himself her hull would be scraped. *Galicia* was now just over a half-mile distant. The sloop nearest her was less than a quarter-mile from her stern.

"Fire in succession!" Donland ordered.

The order was passed and the first gun boomed. Donland watched for the fall of the shot and saw it splash down well in front of the forward sloop.

No more than fifteen seconds passed until the second gun boomed. The shot crashed through the sloop's fore-top sails and rigging. As Donland watched, the yards and sails sagged and then silently draped themselves over the sloop's larboard side.

Oxford's company began to cheer but Powell was quick to put a stop to it. "Blast your eyes and arses, tend to your duties!"

The draping sails acted as an anchor and caused the way to come off the wounded sloop and broach to starboard. Andrews had the range of her and his third shot crashed into her hull just above the water-line.

Oxford's company again began a cheer and Powell allowed it. *Galicia* was no more than a quarter-mile from *Oxford*.

The next boom from Andrews' guns surprised Donland. He quickly lifted the glass but did not see the fall of the shot. To his surprise, when he trained the glass on the second sloop her top'sl yard slowly tilted forward and then pitched into the sea. He heard the cheering from Galicia's crew.

"Secure the guns!" Donland ordered. He did not want to sink either sloop until he knew more of why they were giving chase.

"Prepare to heave-to Mister Powell!" Donland shouted.

Galicia surged forward and was almost abeam of *Oxford*. She was not slowing. Donland lifted the glass to his eye and focused on each officer, Lieutenant Hernandez's face was twisted as he shouted orders. There was no captain on the quarterdeck, either Captain Quadra was injured or dead. Hernandez was definitely in command. Sensing danger he ordered, "Hard to larboard Mister Winslow! Now!"

Winslow obeyed and shouted to the helmsmen, "Hard over larboard!" He did not wait for the helmsmen to respond but launched himself to the wheel and used all his strength to haul the wheel to larboard. The effect was almost immediate; *Oxford* came up into the wind.

Powell became as a wild man shouting one order after another to keep the wind in *Oxford's* sails.

"West by nor'west, Mister Winslow!" Donland shouted just as *Galicia's* ports opened and her lower deck guns ran out. *Oxford* was well into her turn as *Galicia's* guns belched fire and balls. Three balls slammed in *Oxford's* gun-deck just under Donland's feet. The force of the blows caused him to stagger and grasp the railing. "Rudder?" He called to Winslow.

"Answering, Captain!" Winslow called back.

Donland shouted to Brunson, "Mister Brunson, go below and see to our wounded and the damage!"

Galicia's stern was well past, Donland studied her rigging for a moment and concluded that her damage was greater than he had previously thought. Men were busy in her tops mending sail and repairing lines. Even so, it was not so severe as to allow her to turn to starboard and rake *Oxford*.

"Mister Winslow, hard to starboard, bring us round!"

"Aye, Captain!" Winslow answered. He added, "She'll be in irons!"

"Aye! Better in irons than shot through!" Donland acknowledged.

He shouted to Powell, "We're to go round to starboard, ready the braces and yards!"

"Aye, Captain!" Powell replied.

Donland turned his attention to the sloops. Neither was giving chase and were content to watch the drama playing out between the larger ships. Both sloops were occupied with repairs.

Galícia to Donland's surprise, did not alter course but continued west.

Oxford's sails began to flap wildly as they lost the wind.

"Belay Mister Winslow, close hauled!"

Winslow answered, "Aye Captain," as he pulled on the spindles to halt the turn.

"Close hauled!" Donland shouted to Powell.

"Aye, Captain!" Powell replied and began shouting orders to those in the tops and to those on deck manning the lines to haul braces and yards.

Donland again checked on *Galícia*, she was maintaining her course. He continued to watch her until *Oxford's* sails again filled. Turning, he sought out the sloops. They were lying-to still making repairs. Donland understood the lack of their haste, *Galícia* would be resuming her course to her original destination once she was out of range.

The sloops were no more than a half mile distant.

"Mister Brunson, we will heave-to!" Donland shouted to Brunson.

Oxford's way came off her as the main'ls, fors'ls and mizzen were hauled up.

"Brace yards!" Powell shouted and was heard up and down the deck.

"Brace cross-jack square!"

Donland ordered, "Helm a-lee!"

"Aye, Captain," Winslow answered.

There remained some flapping of sail and blocks knocking but all in all *Oxford* came to rest and bobbed upon the swells. "I'll have the jolly boat swayed out Mister Brunson, if you please!" Donland ordered.

Brunson came up the hatch to the quarterdeck and reported, "Main cabin has manageable damage, wardroom and bread room scuttle will give the carpenter and his mates a week's work. Doctor Linn reports two men with small splinters."

"We were fortunate," Donland said. He added, "I shall go across to the nearest sloop. Keep watch on *Galicia* and warn me if she goes about."

"Shall I have the launch swayed out for the Lieutenant Sharpe and the marines?" Powell asked.

"I think not, four men and the jolly boat if you please. I believe we have been duped as to who is the villain. My intention is to offer *Oxford* to assist in the capture or destruction of *Galicia* and to hang Fernandez for piracy." Donland said.

"Sir, it is a risk you should not undertake, allow me to go instead," Powell pleaded.

Donland grinned, "Thank you, for your concern but I believe I have nothing to fear. The jolly boat if you please."

"Aye, Captain," Powell relented.

The jolly boat made fast to the sloop's hull. Men armed with muskets greeted Donland and David as they climbed across the gunnel.

Donland doffed his hat in salute to the Spanish flag. A man wearing a captain's uniform and holding his sword at the ready, stepped forward from those on the small quarterdeck.

As he approached, Donland took in the damage *Oxford* and *Galicia* had inflicted on the sloop.

"I'm Captain Isaac Donland of his majesty's *Oxford*," Donland announced.

"You've discovered you were played for a fool," the Spanish captain stated in perfect English.

Donland replied, "Aye, a Lieutenant Hernandez played his role to perfection. Do I have the honor of addressing Captain Quadra?"

"I am Captain Quadra and I am well acquainted with you Captain Donland. I would that we were not meeting under such circumstances. But, I must ask, why have you come, surely not for my surrender."

Donland answered, "I have come to place myself and my ship at your disposal so that Hernandez might be apprehended." Quadra's face displayed first surprise and then suspicion. "Captain Donland I thank you for your generous offer but this is none of your affair. This is a matter to be settled by my people, Henandez . . ."

Donland cut him off before he could go into more explanation. "Captain Quadra I am offering you command of my vessel and you may bring aboard every man you can muster. I have a small company, no more than eighty men and boys. If you desire to exact revenge on Hernandez, I am giving you the means to do so."

Quadra exclaimed, "Such an act is unheard of!"

"Aye, it is but my desire to see Hernandez sunk or hung is that strong. Gather your men and bring them aboard, I will remain with you as a hostage to ensure your safety."

Donland was mindful that every ear aboard was straining to hear and understand the conversation. He added for their hearing, "I surrender my sword to you." He then drew his sword and offered it to Quadra.

"Captain Donland put away your sword, I'll not accept it. You and I have opposed one another on occasion in these waters several times. Each time you have eluded me and often at great cost to my command. But, you have proven yourself time again to be a just man, one of honor. I beg of you, do not disappoint me."

Donland smiled, "Let us be away before *Galicia* knows what we are about. You have my solemn word, that I mean no harm to you or to your command. *Oxford* will be under your command until Hernandez is taken and then you may go as you please."

"I accept your assistance and your willingness to grant me command but it would not bode well for you if I accept. Let me propose that you retain command and control of your vessel and I shall command my men. Between us we have sufficient men to manage sail and cannon. If it is agreeable to you, I will station my men to the foremast and the mizzen. Your men can continue in their stations on the mainmast. The remainder of our men will go below and drill with the cannon."

"Your proposal is acceptable, however the drill must be without powder and shot for I carry precious little, it is peacetime."

"Yes, of course, peace has come and with it consequences. Nonetheless, let us as you say, be away," Quadra said.

He turned to his lieutenant and spoke in Spainish, "Leave only enough men to keep watch, the rest are to take to the boats. Signal, *La Rosa* to do likewise. Also, bring as much powder and shot as the boats can carry."

Donland signaled *Oxford's* boats to come across to aid in the transfer of the Dons. The combined companies numbered three-hundred and ten. Quadra said the number would more than match that of *Galicia's* company.

"Now it's only a matter of catching up to her. Do you know where she is bound?"

"Yes, Fernandez is to rendezvous with a French vessel off Colombia near Cartagena. Her cargo is to be unloaded and *Galicia* is to be sunk. The tale is to be that she encountered a storm and sank."

Donland considered Quadra's answer. He reasoned that Fernández struck a deal with the French for the gold and silver *Galicia* was carrying. Quadra was careful to say cargo and not gold and silver. He decided not to inquire. The decision to insert himself and *Oxford* into this Spanish matter troubled him. Before putting *Oxford* under the guns of *Galicia*, he would know more of the French intentions. He told himself it might simply be nothing more than piracy, but then it could be a plot to aid a French revolution. No matter which was the case, his only intent was to pursue Hernandez.

Transferring the men, power and shot took the better part of two hours. Donland's first order upon returning to *Oxford* was to send two men as high up the main mast as they could climb. "Each of you take a glass and keep watch on the Spanish two-decker. Call down if she tacks!"

"Aye, Captain!" the two answered and began climbing the shrouds.

"Captain Donland may I suggest we pair our officers so there is no time lost in translating orders," Quadra suggested.

"Aye, an excellent suggestion Captain Quadra," Donland responded. "Please see to the placement of your men and we shall get the ship underway."

Quadra asked, "Have you good men as lookouts, I'd not care to lose *Galicia*?"

"Two good men with sharp eyes with telescopes, there, as high as they can climb," Donland said while pointing.

He cupped his hands and called up, "Masthead? Where away?"

Bill Freedman, one of the two called down, "ship!" and pointed south-east.

Watson, a young seaman called down, "Four miles!"

"She has made her tack and she'll reach the rendezvous well before us," Quadra said with disappointment.

"Aye, but she'll have to transfer the cargo and that will take time, we will catch her and the Frenchman. We've the manpower, the powder and shot to stand against any two our size," Donland said to dispel Quadra's disappointment.

"You will stand against the two?" Quadra asked. His question betrayed his surprise.

Donland smiled and answered, "Aye, I've no doubt of victory."

"Perhaps that is why I was the slow hound and you the elusive fox. My experience and cautious nature was no match for your confidence."

"And there was luck, more than I dare admit to having," Donland replied. He studied his counterpart for a moment then said, "When I fired on the sloops, I did so under the assumption they were pirates. Now, that I know that they are not pirates and *Galicia* are vessels of your majesty's government my hands are tied. Do you have a solution to this dilemma?"

Quadra did not immediately reply then understood the reason for Donland's question. He laughed and said, "I and my king would interpret firing on any Spanish vessel to be an act of war. Having already done so in defense of your vessel was forgiveable but to chase down *Galicia* and seek to destroy her would be viewed as an indefensible act of war." He paused then asked, "But, if you were under my orders and sailed under the flag of Spain, then you would not be held to accounts."

"Aye, you understand my dilemma," Donland replied.

"Then, Captain Donland I give you my permission to hoist the flag of Spain, have you such?"

"Aye, as I am certain that somewhere aboard *Galicia* there is stowed an English flag. But, that is none of my affair."

"Mister Welles, haul down the ensign and run up the Spaniard's flag!" Donland ordered.

"Aye, Captain!" David answered.

Chapter Fourteen

Donland stood with his hands clamped to the railing. Beside him Quadra stood smoking a thick long cigar. The wind, what there was of it, blew the smoke across *Oxford's* stern. Both men could feel the rumble of the heavy guns being run in and out as the gun crews practiced.

"They are working well together, no?" Quadra asked between puffs.

"Aye, as are those aloft," Donland agreed.

Their conversation was interrupted by a hail from the mast. "Her wind has died!"

Donland turned from the railing, "Mister Winslow, what of our wind?"

The sailing master slid from his perch on a sea chest. "How far from shore is she?"

Donland pulled a glass from the rack and focused on *Galicia*, "three miles, I'd estimate. She's that ahead!"

"Be better wind to larboard, she's caught between a land wind and and the trades."

"Mister Powell, we will tack to larboard!" Donland ordered.

"Aye, Captain!" Powell replied and bellowed, "larboard tack!"

The other lieutenants repeated the order, "Larboard tack!" The order was repeated by the Spanish officers.

"Ready about!" Powell bellowed, and the order echoed.

"Hands to bowlines!"

"Tacks and sheets! Lively there Mister Malcolm!"

"Clew garnets!"

"Helm hard to larboard!" Donland ordered and Winslow repeated.

Oxford with the combination of rudder and sail began a slow turn, catching the wind coming from the bows on, her deck tilted sharply.

"Hold her!" Donland called and Winslow repeated.

"Aye," Winslow replied.

Oxford surged northward, there was an occasional flap of a sail.

"*Galicia* still has no wind," Quadra observed.

Donland did not look. He was intent on the sea ahead, studying the eddies of wind on the surface. "If we lose the wind as she has, we've little chance."

"That is so," Quadra said with a hint of despair.

"Four points larboard if you please, Mister Winslow," Donland called.

Winslow replied, "Aye, Captain!"

Oxford gained a knot. Donland turned and judged the distance to the land, four miles he reasoned. "Steady on!" he called.

"Aye, Captain!" Winslow answered.

The heavy guns continued to rumble down below on the gun-deck. Andrews was taking advantage of the tack to work the crews under difficult circumstances. If ordered to run out during an engagement the English and Spanish crews would be better prepared. Donland approved of the young lieutenant's efforts.

Six bells rang out and David called, "The glass is turned!"

Donland called, "Mister Welles instruct the cook to prepare to serve dinner!"

"Aye, Captain," David answered.

"Is that wise?" Quadra asked.

"Men with full bellies will tend their tasks and not be surly, whereas those with empty bellies will be belligerent and slow to obey. As long as the wind remains as it is, we've time to eat. Once we turn east, if we have wind and *Galicia* still lies in doldrums, our afternoon will be eventful. Better the men have their dinner now."

Quadra nodded with understanding.

"We will hold this course then come about and run down to *Galicia*," Donland said.

Seven bells clanged and men began scurrying down the ratlines and shrouds. Donland explained to Quadra, "They will eat by divisions. I see your men are not shy."

Quadra ginned, "They may not relish your English fare."

"Perhaps not, but hunger is the only alternative," Donland said and added, "Once they are fed we shall test the wind."

He jerked a glass from the rack and trained it on *Galicia*. "She is still becalmed," he said. Scanning the sea and then to landward he said, "she will have wind soon."

Quadra was alarmed. "Then we must not delay, every moment we continue northeast we are further away while she sails closer to the French."

Donland explained, "She will have light airs and will barely have steerage whereas we will be able to use the trades to our advantage. Tacking east by south *Oxford* will manage close to if not exceed two knots. *Galicia* may sail at a knot or less. Even if she arrives at her destination before us, she will be within range of our guns."

"Providing we too do not encounter the doldrums," Quadra said with irritation.

"See there," Donland said pointing out to sea at a slight discoloration of the sea surface, "the wind is easterly, veering a bit from the north. That my friend is what will doom Hernandez."

The last of the hands finished their dinner and received their tots of rum. Donland having consumed a biscuit ladened with a chunk of salt pork, took a glass from the rack and found *Galicia*, She was continuing as before, close-hauled. Her top'sls appeared hard and pressed but her lower sails seemed less so. At least he hoped what he saw was true and not just wishful thinking.

He called to Powell, "Mister Powell, we will go about to starboard!"

"Aye, Captain!" Powell answered.

Quadra stood with a telescope to his eye while *Oxford* changed her course. "She continues as before," he said.

"Deck there!" the lookout called down. "Sail east of the two-decker!"

Donland again put the glass to his eye and searched ahead of *Galicia*. He did not see the reported sail.

"I don't see her," Quadra said.

"Nor I," Donland answered.

The rumble of the guns beneath their feet continued. The time for Andrews to prove their worth was drawing near.

Donland considered casting the log but thought better of it. Doing so, were it not to Quadra's expectations could pose needless concern.

"Beat to quarters, if you please Mister Powell," Donland ordered.

Powell bellowed the order, immediately the marine with the drum began the staccato beating. Shrill whistle blasts filled the air as the bosun and his mates sent men to their stations. Overhead, the slings were being slung.

"How far ahead is she?" Quadra asked.

"Two and a half miles, I would estimate. Perhaps in range in a half-hour," Donland answered amidst the chaos of the ship clearing for action.

"I make her speed still as no more than a knot, and ours at better than two," Donland added for measure. He asked, "what is *Galícia's* armament?"

"The upper deck has eighteen, as you say, long nines and the lower deck carries twenty-four eighteen-pound cannon. She was rebuilt for speed and cargo so the armament is to fight off pirates."

"Cargo?" Donland asked.

Donland did not miss Quadra's face clouding.

"Supplies for the colonies from Spain and whatever the colonists produced," Quadra answered.

"Gold and silver?" Donland asked.

"Sometimes, but not always," Quadra hedged.

Donland had his answer, he did not press Quadra.

Oxford was close-hauled and with the wind veering slightly from the north, her deck was tilted to starboard.

Donland lowered his glass, "Mister Winslow, how long can we hold this course?"

"Twenty minutes!" Winslow stated, "More than that and we'll not be able to beat back without going about!"

Donland calculated time, distance and wind. He said to Quadra, "We'll be less than a mile on her stern."

"Mister Powell, I'll have two twelves spiked round to the bow!" Donland ordered.

"Aye, Captain," Powell answered and started for the bow.

"Captain Quadra have you a competent gunner for those two guns?" Donland asked.

"Si!" Quadra answered and called to his lieutenant.

Donland managed a few words in Spainish, enough to make out that Quadra had ordered the lieutenant to assign another officer to the task and to choose his men.

"It is a wise decision to place my men so, firing on their own countrymen is better than your countrymen doing so."

Several minutes passed as the guns were readied. Winslow called to Donland, "Captain we should alter course."

Donland replied, "Aye, Mister Winslow, bring us onto her wake."

"Helm to larboard five points!" Winslow called to the two helmsmen.

"Captain Quadra, you may fire when the guns bear. I am going onto the poop above to see what the Frenchman intends," Donland said as he put a hand on the poop railing.

Three dozen men were arrayed on the poop manning the six-pounders, swivels or armed with muskets. Donland put the glass to his eye and found *Galicia*, he stepped closer to the middle gun and put the glass to his eye again. The Frenchman leaped into view, a frigate. She was on a converging course to *Galicia*. With the wind up her coattails she would reach *Galicia* within minutes. He knew he could not fire on her without provocation but there was nothing stopping Quadra from firing on *Galicia* and if the Frenchman chose to defend her, she would feel the weight of *Oxford's* iron.

One of the twelve-pounders boomed from *Oxford's* bow. By the time Donland reached the stairs to descend the poop, the second gun fired.

"The French are closing on *Galicia*, it will be interesting to see what he intends," Donland said to Quadra

"If he puts himself between us and *Galicia*, I will hit him. Do you object?" Quadra asked.

"It will be logged as an accident. Your ship is only a half mile ahead, your gunner should hit her with his next shot. The

Frechman, if he does not haul his wind will be in danger," Donland answered.

"Mister Powell, I'll have all guns loaded, if you please!"

"Aye, Captain, Powell called from the waist.

Donland turned back to Quadra, "The French captain will not know that this is an English ship. He will see the flag of Spain and not hesitate to decimate us if he can. I expect he will luff when he is abeam of *Galicia*, broach to present his guns and *Galicia* will do likewise. Our advantage is that Hernandez will not know we have both companies from the sloops. When he was aboard, he could not help but to notice my depleted company."

"You intend to sail between them?" Quadra asked.

Donland answered, "If both captains are of a mind to do as I predicted, yes. Fernandez will expect *Oxford* to turn to starboard to avoid the Frenchman's guns. The Frenchman will expect our turn to be to larboard and will have his starboard battery loaded with grape."

"It is the French way, disable and then as you say, pound into submission," Quadra said with a faint smile.

"Aye, it is the way of the French. I suspect that is one of the newer frigates. You've no doubt noticed? She may be carrying carronades on her deck, possibly equipped with those new bombs I've heard about. If she is so armed, were we to do as he expects, it would be disastrous."

"So you choose to split them and thus avoid his guns and carronades?" Quadra asked. His voice betrayed his admiration of Donland's plan. He said, "The wily fox does again what is not expected."

The lookout hailed the deck, "Frenchman spilled her wind!" Donland lifted the glass, indeed the French captain had spilled his wind and was turning to larboard. He was backing his sails. Checking *Galicia*, he saw that she too was spilling her wind and turning to starboard.

"They've set their trap," Quadra who also had a glass to his eye commented.

"Mister Winslow, we will pass between them! Another set of arms on the wheel, if you please!" Donland shouted.

Oxford was yet a quarter-mile from the trap. The Spaniards firing the twelve-pounders sent up a cheer as a ball tore through *Galicia's* rigging.

"All guns loaded, Captain! Shall I run out?" Powell called.

"Not yet Mister Powell, we will pass between those two! When the Frenchman fires, open ports! Pass the word, fire when there's a target!"

"Aye, Captain!" Powell answered.

The lookout called down, "Ports opening!"

Donland said to Quadra, "the Frechman will hold fire until he sees us turn as will Fernandez. They'll not know what to do until we make a move."

"Perhaps a feint toward one or the other? Such a move may add to their confusion."

"We've not the wind, had we more it would be in order but as it is, we best proceed and have them questioning our intentions. Your Hernandez, does he have experience in command?"

Quadra laughed then said, "The man is an ideological fool. He has less time at sea than that boy yonder, he knows nothing of tactics. He comes from a family of politicians."

"Then he will not suspect what we are about," Donland said and added. "The Frechman behaves as a man of little experience or else he is very cunning. We'll know very soon."

"We've less than four hundred yards," Quadra said. Donland sensed the man was holding his breath, waiting for the explosions to come.

Oxford became as quiet as a cemetery at midnight. Only the natural sounds of wind, the splash of waves against the hull and the creaking of the ship could be heard. Quadra wasn't the only one holding his breath.

The twelve-pounders fired again in unison striking solid blows against *Galicia's* hull. Donland imaged the carnage the balls wrought as they burst through the hull showering the men with daggers of splinters

Oxford was only a hundred yards from the two ships. There was nothing they could do to prevent *Oxford* sailing between them. Both Hernandez and the French captain, no doubt, realized their mistake. It was too late for them to wedge guns around or to move either ship so that their guns would bear.

A burst of smoke erupted from the French frigate's deck. It was followed by a second burst of smoke. Two balls splashed alongside *Oxford's* hull signaling misses. The sudden explosions surprised Donland. His mind registered the events. *Bombs!*

Now he knew why the French captain was biding his time and understood the man's cunning. He called up to the fighting top where Lieutenant Sharpe commanded his marines, "Target those bomb crews! Hit them!"

"Aye, Captain!" Sharpe answered.

Several musket shots followed his order.

He turned his attention to the next danger. "Mister Powell!" Donland shouted, his voice sounded like thunder in the quiet while the marines reloaded their muskets. "Starboard guns! Full elevation!"

"Aye, Captain!" "Starboard guns full elevation!" Powell answered. He need not have for the starboard gun crews would have heard Donland's order.

No sooner were the words out of Donland's mouth than there was another burst of musket fire from the frigate's marines. Muskets began to bang from the Spaniard's tops.

"Top's'l's only Mister Powell!" Donland shouted.

A sudden explosion ripped across the Frenchman's deck. Sharpe's marines began to cheer. Donland saw flames on the frigate's decks and men rushing with buckets to douse the fire. The cheering, Donland realized, was because one of the marine's shots had dropped a man holding a lighted bomb about to be inserted into the cannon.

"Well done Mister Sharpe, now mark down those in the tops!"

"Aye, Captain!" Sharpe answered and ordered his marines in the next breath, "Fire!"

The swivels and six-pounders on the poop deck did not wait for orders but fired on their own. Swivels and small cannon aboard the frigate answered their fire. *Oxford's* deck sizzled as musket balls and canister balls flew through the air sending small splinters flying. Two men working the waist went down amid cries of pain.

The French frigate fired four of her main guns, it was a waste of power and shot as the balls fell well behind *Oxford*. The same held true for when Hernandez ordered all his guns to fire. *Oxford* was unscathed. Her bowsprit was now passing between the two ships.

Boom! The first of *Oxford's* larboard thirty-two pound guns fired. The crash of the ball was almost immediate. It tore through the frigate's bow like a knife through butter. The screams of the wounded and dying filled the air.

The second shot from the larboard cannon tore through the hole its predecessor had made. Adding to the death and destruction.

Boom! The starboard gun fired and was answered by its nearby mate. The first ball tore through the upper part of *Galicia's* stern and continued onward into her mizzen. The second ball cleared the stern and banged hard into the mizzen mast, it immediately began to tilt and in slow motion carried away sails, rigging and tackle.

Boom! Boom! Boom! Boom! The four shots were in quick succession. Donland and Quadra stood anchored to *Oxford's* quarterdeck in mystified horror of the carnage. Muskets still banged and balls splat around the quarterdeck as the French marksmen tried to mark down Donland. There was a horrific scream as one of the French musket men was hit and fell from the fighting top to crash onto the deck near the French captain.

Donland's attention was drawn to the French captain, he could see the man's face, their eyes met across the distance. Suddenly the French captain drew his sword, the man was almost knocked off his feet as two more thirty-two pound balls crashed into his bow. The captain pulled his handkerchief and tied it to his sword and held it high meeting Donland's eyes.

"Cease firing!" Donland shouted.

Two more guns from the starboard battery fired. Then all became quiet.

Oxford's foremast was now even with the Frenchman's stern. Donland lost sight of the French captain as the Frenchman's poop obscured his view. He turned to see what damage was wrought on *Galicia*, she was missing her mizzen, part of her main and only her foremast remained intact.

"I've wrecked your ship," Donland said and realized Quadra was sitting on the deck. The man's hand was covered in blood as he pressed it against his bleeding left leg.

Quadra stared up at Donland and grinned. "Yes, and perhaps my leg as well but it is a glorious victory, your victory."

Donland did not respond but ordered, "Mister Welles, get some men and take the captain below to the surgeon!"

"Not yet," Quadra said. "The wound is minor, I would see my ship!"

"Help him to his feet Mister Welles," Donland ordered.

All firing had stopped. Donland called to Powell, "Spill our wind!"

"Aye, Captain," Powell answered.

"Grapples!" Donland ordered. "Starboard and larboard!"

"Mister Winslow, I mean to lie-to between the two!"

Winslow grinned and replied, "Aye, Captain!"

The grapples were thrown across to the stern of *Galicia* and to the bow of the French frigate. None were thrown off or cut.

"Mister Powell, pass the word to the guns! They are to standby but not stand-down!"

"Aye, Captain," Powell answered and then asked, "Boats?"

130

"Aye," Donland answered. "All boats in the water, if you please Mister Powell."

"Aye, Captain," Powell answered.

Donland turned to face Quadra who was on his feet. "How is it with you?"

"Bleeding is but a trickle, the ball only tore my britches and a bit of flesh. I would see my ship."

"I'll have three boats in the water, load them with your men and send one of your lieutenants to take possession of *Galicia*. Have him warn those aboard that if a shot is fired, I will send them to the bottom!"

"Captain Donland, you have been more than gracious and I am greatly in your debt but my first duty is to my ship," Quadra replied and limped from the quarterdeck.

"Captain Quadra, there is the matter of the French frigate, I can not nor can my men go aboard her. She has surrendered and her captain awaits you. Let me urge you sir, send your lieutenant to *Galicia* and you attend the French captain."

Quadra stopped and turned back to Donland, "What you said is so. I shall attend the Frenchman, perhaps I shall gain answers to questions that have thus far eluded me."

"Mister Welles, tally our wounded and report back to me. I am going onto the poop," Donland ordered.

Sergeant Hawkes saluted Donland as he stepped onto the poop. He asked Hawkes, "What of the Spaniards?"

"Tending their wounded Captain Donland, we gave them fair hell!"

"Did you hit any officers?"

"Aye, Captain, one canister of grape cut them all down, went down like a scythe cutting hay. The lads cheered like hyenas, so they did. See there, Captain," Hawkes said and pointed toward the Spaniard's deck.

Donland found it difficult to make out very much on the deck as most of it was covered in downed rigging and canvas. He could hear the cries of dying men. A few men were moving about, mostly they were attempting to free their mates who were pinned. He saw no officers.

"They'll not trouble us further," He said as much to Hawkes as to himself. "Well done, Sergeant, have you wounded?"

"None of mine. A couple of the Dons were killed out right," Hawkes answered.

"The French have shown the white flag but until we know that that both vessels are under Captain Quadra's command, we will not stand down."

"Aye, Captain," Hawkes said with a large grin. He added, "Will make them beg if they so much as sneeze wrong."

Chapter Fifteen

Donland returned to the quarterdeck and was met by Powell. "Will you go across and accept the Frenchman's sword and surrender?"

"No, Mister Powell, Captain Quadra commands, we are under his flag. He is now on his way to the Frenchman."

"But, Sir," Powell began.

Donland cut him off, "There is not a but, Mister Powell, for me to accept the surrender would place England in a difficult position with the French. Their lordships would have my hide as well as yours. So no, I will not venture across to the frigate and neither is any of our company to do so. I believe it would be wise to pass the word that any man who utters a word across the gulf be told that their backsides will be forfeit."

"Aye, Captain, I understand and will pass the word."

"Beg pardon, Captain," Welles said.

"What is it Mister Welles?"

"You asked about the wounded, nine wounded but not severely. Six of the dons are dead and another eighteen are wounded."

"Thank you, Mister Welles," Donland said.

"We fared well," Powell said to Donland.

"Aye, were it not for Lieutenant Sharpe's marksmanship I fear the bombs may have caused us great damage."

"Carronades and bombs, I'd not expected such," Powell said.

"Prudent would you not say, if you are carrying gold and silver? Pirates would have little chance of boarding her," Donland said.

"I'd not want to face those smashers and bombs. Had I known they were aboard, I'd have prayed a little longer and a little harder," Powell said and grinned.

"Aye, as we all would have done." Donland agreed.

"Captain, the wind is freshening, we'll not be able to linger here much longer," Winslow advised.

"A few minutes longer, Mister Winslow. We'll not move until it is safe to do so," Donland said.

He turned back to Powell, "Once Captain Quadra is in possession of both vessels, we will be away to the south to make contact with the sloops. He will need help with repairs to his ship. The Frenchman is his to sort out. It is to our good to stay out of that entanglement."

"Our company will be disappointed not to have her as a prize. Some have already counted their share."

Donland half-smiled and said, "Just as they've already tasted their next tot of grog. But, if they knew the choice was between prize money and employment, I think they would choose employment. The beach is not for men such as these nor for such as you and I."

"I'll be sure the word makes the rounds," Powell added. He was about to add more but the flag aboard the frigate was coming down.

Donland noticed that Powell's attention was focused elsewhere, so he turned to see the Spanish flag hoisted. "Have the grapples cut, if you please Mister Powell," he said with satisfaction.

"Aye, Captain and will we be getting underway?" Powell asked.

"Top'sl for now and steerage enough to maneuver. I will go across to *Galicia*," Donland answered.

The smell of death greeted Donland as he came over *Galicia's* gunnel. He made his way past a man lying on his back against a coil of rope. The splinter in the man's chest was as large as marlinespike.

Doctor Linn knelt beside the man, examined the wound and stood. He shook his head, signaling the man's time was near. He rose and went in search of the next victim.

Quadra stood on what remained of his quarterdeck giving orders in rapid Spanish. He saw Donland and stepped away from his officers.

"Captain Donland, you indeed did wreck my ship but even so I am grateful to have her returned to me," Quadra said and smiled.

"I've brought my surgeon, have you one aboard."

"Yes, I've a physician, he is below sawing limbs. Capable man, but of little use for such wounds." He changed tack and asked, "What do you intend?"

"The Frenchman is in your lieutenant's hands. I suggest you send sufficient men across to aid him. I can not board her for reasons I'm sure you understand."

"Yes, yes, of course, your country has no part in this affair. As to the ship, I am going to release her. A good faith gesture, I think you would call it."

"Her captain?" Donland asked.

"He, I will hold until I have the answers I seek. His part and his government's part will go in my report to my king. These traitors will be hung." Quadra said, indicating two bound men sitting on the deck.

"Fernandez, did he survive?" Donland asked.

"No, the curr died before I came aboard. It was better for him to die from a musketball than from my sword for I would have showed no mercy." Quadra spit on the deck for emphasis.

"*Oxford* is about to sail south and rendezvous with your sloops. Perhaps you can spare one of your officers to sail with me. Those aboard would trust his word more than mine."

"Yes, I shall send Lieutenant Jose Camacho, he commands the sloop *San Felipe*. I shall also send across enough men to sail the sloops. You will in any case need your boats returned."

"Then I shall be away. It has been my pleasure to assist you and to serve with you," Donland said.

"The pleasure, Captain Donland has been all mine. Were it not for your intervention, my ship and my honor would be lost to me. I will always hold you in great esteem and always count you as a friend even if, due to the foolishness of our countrymen, we find ourselves opposing one another."

"Aye," Donland said and put out his hand.

Quadra took Donland's hand and pulled him close and embraced him.

As they separated, Donland searched for Doctor Linn. Not seeing him, he said to Quadra, "My surgeon is somewhere about, please send a man to locate him that we may return to our ship."

Quadra turned and spied a young man wearing an officer's uniform. "Fetch the English doctor, he is to return," Quadra ordered.

"Si, Capitan," the young officer answered and set off.

Donland climbed down into the boat.

It was several minutes before Linn's head appeared above him. He then hurriedly descended the rope ladder to the boat. "Many will live and there are many that will not," Linn stated.

"What of the Spanish surgeon?" Donland asked as the boat began to pull away.

"Fair enough, but he can do no more than I."

The two sloops sat bobbing on the rolling waves. The few men aboard each sloop had made good use of their time to effect repairs. Lieutenant Camacho spoke no English but smiled broadly and saluted Donland upon leaving *Oxford*.

"So it ends," Donland said as Camacho exited through the sally port.

"Aye, Captain and a great victory for you. The tale of how you defeated both a French fleet and a Spanish fleet will be told in every ale house in these waters," Powell ventured.

"Thankfully, it will not be believed, else I'll have to answer to a board of inquiry."

"I did as you asked and had our juniors minimize events in their personal logs. They understood the need for doing so. I did, however, give them permission to enter simply that we rendered assistance to a Spanish vessel that was beset by pirates. They will be sure to enter certain heroics."

"Aye, as I'm sure you will," Donland said as he clapped Powell on the shoulder.

"Aye, Captain, Aye," Powell replied.

Chapter Sixteen

"Tack to larboard!" Powell ordered.

Donland heard the order and pulled his watch. It was the third time they had tacked in four hours. Winslow stated that it was unusual for the wind to be from the north this time of the year. He also stated that the sea was as flat as he had ever seen and disliked the strange hue of blue-green.

The heat in the cabin was oppressive, the water in the pitcher did little to quench his thirst. Even with the cabin door propped open there was only a faint breeze blowing through the cabin.

"Pity the poor sailor," Honest said as he stirred from the chair in which he lounged. "I'm for the orlop deck, there be a missing platter the lads did not return when we set-to with that Frenchie."

"Aye," Donland said absentmindedly. His mind was still on setting down the details of aiding Quadra. It was his fourth draft of the affair and he was having difficulty with a feasible explanation of his involvement. Pettibone would not be pleased to read the account without a clear statement of why it was necessary to aid the Spaniard. But it was not Pettibone that gave him concern, no it was the clerks sitting in some dungeon of an office in the admiralty. He was certain they were instructed to flag reports involving Spanish or French encounters. Sumerford had said as much during one of their conversations. The information that he often acted on came from an obscure report either from a naval officer or an army officer. "Write nothing that will incur scrutiny," Sumerford had said.

A knock sounded at the door. Seeing the woman and her son, he barked, "Enter!"

Rosita pushed her son into the office. "Beg pardon, sir, but I'm to ask what is to be done with us?"

Donland laid aside his quill, studied the woman. He'd not given thought to the married women since off the coast of Panama. In fact he had forgotten they were still aboard. "You know we are bound for Port Royal, once there you will be sent ashore along with the other woman. Your man and son have signed into the muster book and are thus obligated. I could, in good conscience, set them ashore or punish them. I could also have you whipped for signing on as a man. Understand I have options and there is no one to question my decision. But, aside from my displeasure there has been no harm, so I shall do as I said, set you ashore. Your husband and the boy will remain."

"I can cook and clean for you, I'll be no bother! I've not been!" she pleaded.

"I've been lenient with you Rosita, you've my answer."

He called, "Sentry!"

The marine sentry stepped into the office and came between Donland and the woman. "Captain?" the marine asked.

"Take these two out!"

"Aye, Captain," The marine replied and turned to the woman. He held his musket across his chest pushed it toward the woman and boy. They retreated through the open door.

Donland was about to begin again composing the account. He heard the step on the deck and looked up. "Mister Powell?"

"All repairs have been made, they depleted our reserve of planking. I've two for the punishment and Mister Andrews is unwell, he's with the surgeon as we speak."

"The two for punishment, what infractions?"

"Both fighting, I'll assign extra duty on the pumps," Powell said.

Donland did not miss the slight glance at the decanter of brandy on the sideboard. He stood and said, "What are their names?"

"Geddins and Archibald, both are of Mister Brunson's watch. He attests to the fight."

Donland lifted the brandy decanter and poured a portion in a goblet, then poured a smaller amount in a second goblet. He took the first and handed it to Powell. "We've earned a drop," he said.

"Aye, earned but not needed," Powell said as he accepted the goblet. "Being at sea again has erased the need."

"I'm delighted to hear that. Before we sailed, I was concerned as well as troubled. You're too fine an officer to allow such to become a distraction."

Donland lifted his goblet, "To *Oxford*."

"Aye, to *Oxford*," Powell said and sipped the brandy.

"Winslow predicts our arrival at about noon," Donland said casually as he returned to his desk.

"Aye, he said as much to me. I can't say that I'll be pleased to return so soon. Truthfully, I would prefer another month afloat."

"Aye, as I but we've proven her sea-worthiness and with that done we may receive our full complement. Perhaps, the commodore will allow us to put her up on the docks. I imagine with her bottom cleaned of weed that she should gain a few knots with a good wind."

Powell sat in one of the chairs and took another sip of brandy. He broached the question, "Will their lordships grant you your step?"

Donland said more confident than he felt, "They'll not refuse the queen's request. Were it not for that, I'd not give it a smattering of a chance."

"We've been fifteen days at sea," Powell said and paused.

Donland added, "Aye, and three months since leaving Antigua. Angermanland is probably back in his country and the queen occupied with balls and hunts. Neither will give thought to a lowly lieutenant on the other side of the world. So, as to the question, in time we shall hear the verdict."

Outside Donland's office the bell clanged once. Mellencamps' boyish voice called, "the glass is turned".

"I've the watch," Powell said and rose from his chair.

"I take it that it was to be Andrews'?" Donland asked.

"Aye, it was," Powell said and placed his goblet back on the sideboard.

"He is an asset to our company. I trust his illness is only temporary. I confess to still being amazed that he came to us with only the barest hope of employment."

"Aye, just as I forsook all for a mere chance of employment. What fools we must be," Powell said and smiled.

"You best attend the watch, and I best attend this report. I've not much time," Donland said preferring that he were the one to go on deck.

The report was finally finished but not to his liking. He drained his glass and was about to refill it, when a knock at the cabin door sounded. He shouted, "Enter!"

"Beg pardon Captain," Aldridge said. "Portland Key off the bow."

"Thank you, Mister Aldridge, I shall be there in a few moments. Who has the watch?"

"Mister Brunson, Captain."

141

"Very good, please inform Mister Powell," Donland said as he stood.

"I'll fetch your hat and sword," Honest said as he picked up the plate and the wineglass.

"Delicious cake, you've improved on your baking," Donland said.

"Not me, it was Rosita," Honest said and disappeared into the galley.

Donland called, "I thought as much, several of my meals were more than you could manage. A decent cook you may be but the seasoning spoke of a woman's touch. Am I correct in my assessment?"

"Here you are, Captain," Honest said as he held out the sword belt.

Donland raised his arms as Honest buckled the belt. "Aye, Sir, you were looking a mite thin, and I thought it best you have better food to regain your strength."

"I thank you for being concerned about my health but I know it to be true that you've spent considerable time below with your mates. Dice, drink and lies are what you were about while she cooked."

"As you are fond of saying, perhaps," Honest joked.

Donland watched as the coast of Jamaica slid by. The white beaches and dense lush jungle gave the appearance of paradise, he knew better. Beyond the white sand were all manner of pests and vermin. He much preferred life aboard to that of the land.

Leeland, the purser, stood off the larboard railing. Donland had come to dislike the man and considered replacing him. The man was distant and withdrawn. Powell reported talking with the man on several occasions and each time came away with few answers. At every turn, Leeland's accounting was a little off. Either the man could not count or he was just bad with figures.

The surgeon, Linn, was a different story. He was bright, energetic and showed great concern for the men's health. Rather

than remaining aloof, he regularly circulated with the men below
deck. And, he was as good a physician as Donland had
encountered.

"Wind holding steady," Winslow observed.

"Two hours?" Donland asked.

"Aye," Winslow answered and sighed heavily.

"I take it that you are not pleased to be returning to Port
Royal," Donland said.

Winslow slid onto the chest on which he sat most of the
time that he was on deck. "The future, Captain Donland is much
like the wind, it can be fickle and difficult to discern its strength
or it can rush on a man like the wind of a hurricane. On the sea,
a man can gauge the future, one day is like another and the
storms can be prepared for beforehand."

"Aye," Donland agreed. He had spent a great deal of time
considering what his future would be once they reached Port
Royal. A letter from the Admiralty was foremost on his mind.
That letter would determine the winds of the future. He
refrained from considering his future if he was denied the
promotion.

The bell rang out, Aldridge called, "The glass is turned."

Dinner, what there was of it was waiting on the men. They
hurried to partake of the burgaboo, ship's biscuits and the dregs
of the grog that remained. Were the cook relying on Leeland's
count, there would be no noon meal this day nor would there be
a ration of grog.

"Take in studding sails!" Powell shouted through his
trumpet. He followed with, "Burtons off the yards; jiggers off
the topgallant yards!"

They were just passing Mosquito Point. Donland knew the
Commodore would have been told of their arrival. He expected
to see, *Captain repair ashore*, flying from the signal mast.

"Man the fore-clew garnets!"

Brunson shouted, "Buntlines and leechlines! Lively there!"

"Mainsail haul!" Powell bellowed.

They were past Mosquito Point. Ahead, were anchored a sixty-four and, two frigates and several smaller vessels. Boats were plying back and forth to the anchored ships. Powell ordered, "Furl sails, haul taut and stop in the rigging!"

Donland felt the sweat trickling down his armpits. *Oxford's* way was coming off her.

"Let go aft!" Powell shouted and the aft anchor descended to the depths without a splash. More than a minute elapsed while the slack in the cable ran out and tugged *Oxford* slightly to starboard. When Powell was satisfied he ordered, "Let go bow!" "Capstan haul!" The cable came taut and *Oxford* was snugged to her anchors.

"Signal Captain, *Captain repair ashore*," Welles said knowing that Donland had seen it.

"Mister Brunson," Donland called. "I'll have the launch, if you please!"

"Aye, Captain," Brunson answered.

Donland bent and picked up the small satchel Honest had set as his feet. Leeland was waiting at the sally port, the men would need their evening meal and the ration of grog.

The boat was lowered; Leeland went through the port first, followed by Hornsby, Brunson then Donland. No one spoke as they were rowed across to the quay.

The marine sentries on the quay stood at attention. Lieutenant Halston was waiting, he saluted and said, "It is good to see you again, sir. The commodore is waiting in his office."

"Thank you, Mister Halston, let us attend the commodore. I have my reports."

"Very good, I trust your voyage was uneventful? We were expecting your return several days ago and the commodore feared *Oxford* lost." Halston said.

"The voyage was not without events, and our delay was due to those events. I will discuss them with the commodore."

"Aye, Captain," Halston replied and did not ask another question or make a comment as they walked to the commodore's residence.

Halston stopped before Pettibone's door and knocked. "Come!" Pettibone answered.

Halston entered first and said, "Captain Donland, sir!" He then backed out of the door and closed it. Donland removed his hat.

"So, you've returned. I feared you lost after the tenth day. I'm sure you have a valid explanation. One that will justify the delay."

"Aye, Commodore, I have," Donland said and opened the satchel. "I've my written reports."

"Please sit, I will get to those afterwards. Do you care for refreshments?"

"Thank you, but no," Donland said as he sat. "As to the delay, I encountered a Spanish cut-down third-rate under fire by two sloops and I presumed them to be pirates. The decision to intervene was made after the Spanish vessel hoisted, in our code, *request assistance*. As *Oxford* drew near, I ordered two guns to fire upon the nearest sloop. One shot hit home and the other missed. The other sloop broke off the engagement and the other limped away. I then made the decision to render aid and to escort the stricken Spaniard to Colon. The winds were contrary and fitful, and the Spaniard, due to his damage had great difficulty."

"What was the name of the ship and the name of the captain?" Pettibone asked.

"Captain Quadra commanding the *Galicia*," Donland answered.

Pettibone smiled and said, "Quadra, a name which I am familiar. A formidable man as I recall. Did you discover that *Galicia* was a treasure ship bound for Spain?"

Donland managed a half smile, "Captain Quadra did not disclose his cargo but it stands to reason that the pirates did not attack in such force for a cargo of sugar-cane."

"Indeed not, but I must ask you if those you suspected of being pirates flew a national flag, perhaps the flag of Spain?"

Donland became concerned. It was evident that Pettibone was aware of the sloops and their nationality. He answered, "Aye, the flag of Spain. I discounted the validity of the flag until after I met with Captain Quadra aboard one of the sloops some time later. He confirmed that *Galicia* was commanded by traitors he suspected were aligned with French revolutionaries."

"Yet, you continued to insert yourself and your ship in Spain's affairs!" Pettibone said with his voice now tinged with anger.

"Aye, for a Lieutenant Hernandez, who was in command of the *Galicia* when *Oxford* arrived, had taken possession of her and later fired on *Oxford*. Before I was aware of the deception I was forced to re-engage the sloops.

"You fought off the sloops knowing that they were in fact legitimate vessels of Spain!" Pettibone exploded. "Did you not realize you were risking war with Spain?"

"Aye, I did!"

Pettibone's face was red with rage. "After all I've done to assist you and now you have placed me in jeopardy of losing all I've gained. Damn you, sir, damn you!"

Donland stood, "I've not placed you in jeopardy! Read the report before you damn me! I'd not do that to you and in my reports you can plainly read that I bear all responsibility and in no way have I alluded to you being complicit. Read my report!"

They glared at each other for a long moment. Pettibone sighed and said, "I will read the report and when I've finished, I will call for you. Return to your ship and await my signal!"

"Aye, sir," Donland said and pulled the reports and the logs from the satchel. He handed them across to Pettibone, Turned and headed for the door.

Chapter Seventeen

Donland was slumped in his chair staring out the transom window. He filled the goblet again. His mind was on the conversation with Pettibone. It had not gone well because Pettibone was already aware of the Spaniard's presence off Panama. How he knew did not matter. What mattered was that he was sorely displeased that *Oxford* was involved.

Honest stood in the galley door polishing the silver and brass hilt of Donald's fancy sword that he wore on special occasions. He was watching Donland, and decided that if Donland started to pour a third goblet of brandy, he would have to stop him. It would not do for Pettibone summon the captain while he was in a drunken state.

There was hard knocking at the quarterdeck door. Donland paid it no heed so Honest ducked into the state-room and made his way to the door to see who was about.

The marine sentry stood blocking the door with his musket across his chest.

"Easy lad," Honest said and the marine stepped aside.

To Honest's great surprise, it was the devil himself waiting to be admitted, Sumerford.

"Be damned!" Honest managed.

"And you should be," Sumerford said. "I'll see the Captain!"

"Aye, but you best not take the bottle. Allow me to have it and I will return it you to present at a more suitable time."

"Is there a problem? Is he ill?" Sumerford asked.

"Come," Honest said and after Sumerford stepped through the door, he closed it and whispered, "Mad as blazes, ornery and drinking!"

"Then I should join him," Sumerford said with a smile.

"I think not, the commodore is to call for him at any time and I would that he be sober."

"Troubles then, is it?"

"Aye, and then some. He's not said much but what he has said lends itself to a blow coming that will sink a sailor."

"Perhaps I should hear it from his lips and sort it," Sumerford said.

"Aye, he'll listen to reason if it comes from you."

Honest pushed open the main cabin door for Sumerford. "A visitor, Captain," he announced.

Donland immediately sat upright and turned. "Mathias!" Donland stood, he was a bit unsteady but managed to regain his balance and extend his hand.

Sumerford smiled broadly, "It is me in the flesh, I'd not miss a chance to come aboard and renew our friendship. They told me that your arrival was delayed. I was beginning to fear the worse. How are you?"

"Truthfully, in torment. But that is not a concern worthy of dampening your arrival. I am so pleased to see you." Before he realized it he asked, "Have you come alone?"

Sumerford drew back and sternly said, "Isaac have I not always come alone, why should my sudden appearance cause such a question?"

Donland replied, "Beg pardon friend, I mean no insult."

Sumerford smiled and said, "None taken, friend, none taken. Although, I can imagine you would prefer that I were another with the name Sumerford. Alas, you will have to content yourself with my presence."

"How is she? Have you heard from her?" Donland asked.

"I have and she is well. She asked me to tell you, should our paths cross, that she thinks fondly of you."

"Aye, and I her," Donland said betraying the gloom of not seeing Betty.

"Take heart old man," Sumerford said. "She has sent me to invite you to dine with her tonight."

Donland's face lit up, "She has accompanied you?"

"No, I have accompanied her. She insisted on making the voyage from Charleston to Antigua. We discovered you were not there and were in fact here. So we booked passage and arrived four days ago. I must tell you that she has been worried because of your late arrival. But, she was determined to stay until either you returned or there was some word of your circumstances."

"You've brought to me the best news I could have hoped for," Donland said. "I would go to her now except I've been ordered to remain aboard until sent for."

"The reason for your drink?" Sumerford asked.

"Aye, the commodore, he's in a right state of agitation. I tried to explain but he is too concerned about his position to listen. I can only hope that after he reads my report that he will understand."

Sumerford patted Donland on the shoulder and said, "I've dined with the man and we've discussed you. He's a fair man and thinks highly of you. I dare say you have not a worry, he'll see the logic in your decisions."

"I trust you are correct in your assessment."

A knocking at the door interrupted them. "Enter!" Donland called.

David came in with his hat in the crook of his arm. He smiled upon seeing Sumerford then remembered his duty. "Captain, a signal from the commodore, you are requested ashore."

"Thank you, David," Donland said and added, "I shall go across, will you accompany me Mathias?"

"With great pleasure," Sumerford said.

Lieutenant Halston opened the door for Donland. Pettibone was sitting behind his desk. He got right to the point. "Please sit, Isaac. I've read your reports and I understand the decisions you made. In your report, you omitted several details that you shared with me earlier. The written report says nothing about the sloops being under Spanish colors nor does it mention that you fought the sloops again. Explain to me why you omit those facts?"

"Before I give the explanation, allow me to complete my oral report. There are other events that I have omitted and I have done so for numerous reasons which I believe will be obvious to you once you've heard all the details. It will be best if only your ears hear what I've to say."

"I've little choice then," Pettibone said. He stood and crossed the room to the door. He opened the door and said to Halston and to the clerk, "Please wait outside on the street until I've my conversation with Captain Donland. See that no one enters."

Halston and the clerk exchanged glances but rose from their desks and entered the hall.

"There will be no one listening. Proceed, if you please."

"As I told you earlier, off the coast of Panama we came upon the three Spanish vessels. Once the sloops were routed, the captain on the *Galicia* came aboard *Oxford*. He thanked me for intervening and then rejoined his ship. He said his name was

Henandez. I thought it odd at the time that he refused further assistance and rejected my surgeon coming aboard to tend his wounded. We lay-to during the night less than a mile apart. Before dawn, we began to get underway. I discovered that *Galicia* was doing like-wise. The two sloops had positioned themselves during the night to intercept *Galicia* and they came at her as she got under way. My intention at the time was to return to Port Royal but upon seeing the renewed threat to *Galicia*, I ordered a change of course to fight off the sloops. I did so successfully, again damaging the sloops. It was then that *Galicia* altered course with the full intention of raking *Oxford*. I had suspected something of the sort, I'm not sure why, so I was able to take evasive action. We received two hits, little damage, but by the time I recovered from the maneuver, *Galicia* was well away. It was then I rendezvoused with the sloops under a flag of truce. Captain Quadra was aboard one of the sloops and he explained that his first lieutenant had mutinied and was sailing to off load the cargo to a French man-of-war."

Pettibone digested the telling of events. He asked, "Did it not occur to you at that point to leave it to the Dons to sort out?"

"It did, sir, but I determined that it was in the crown's interest to assist the Dons. My reasoning was that the mutineers, if in fact they were taking a treasure ship, would do so again and thus enrich those seeking to overthrow the Spanish monarchy as well as the French. England would, in time, face a threat. I also, reasoned that Fernandez would not fear English ships and attack unsuspecting ships that he viewed as a threat." Donland paused to allow Pettibone to ask questions.

"Your reasoning is valid but why not include it in the written report?"

Donland answered, "I could not be sure their lordships would view events in the same light as I did and because of what I saw as my only course of action. Which was, to go across and

meet with Captain Quadra. I offered him command of my ship
for the pursuit of Hernandez and *Galicia.*"

"You what?" Pettibone broke in.

Donland repeated, "I offered him command of *Oxford* but
he refused it."

"Thank God!" Pettibone said with relief.

"In order that my actions not to be viewed as acts of war,
we agreed to hoist the Spanish flag and we ferried the companies
of the sloops to *Oxford.* In essence, Quadra commanded for he
could fire on *Galicia* without it being an act of war. And he could
challenge the Frenchman without involving England. And that is
what occurred. The Frenchman was forced to surrender to
Quadra, not a single Englishman set foot on the Frenchman's
deck and only I and Doctor Linn set foot on *Galicia* for the
purpose of rendering medical aid. For all intents and purposes it
was Captain Quadra's fight and victory."

Donland sat back in the chair. He was exhausted and
wanted a drink.

Pettibone too sat back in his chair and digested the report.
Twice he sat up as to ask a question only to purse his lips and
relax. Finally he asked, "The Frenchman, a frigate or larger?"

"Frigate, one of the newer ones with both carronades and
bombs," Donland answered.

"You fought her and the Spanish two-decker and incurred
no casualties, that sir is hard to believe."

Donland said calmly, "The Spanish lost fewer than ten and
Oxford only a few with wounds that will heal in time."

"How in God's name did you manage such a feat? The
Admiralty will desire that answer and I can assure you they'll not
believe it. Have you any proof?"

Frustrated, Donland replied, "I've no proof other than the
word of my officers. As to the how of the thing, both the Frog
and the Don took positions bow to aft expecting *Oxford* to tack
either to larboard or starboard, instead I ordered that we go
between them. Both left off firing until neither of their guns

would bear. My marines marked down the bomb crews and once in the gap between the Don and the Frog I ordered the Don's masts and rigging targeted and the Frog's bow targeted. Without returning fire, they were soon decimated and forced to surrender."

Pettibone leaned back in his chair. "I understand your written report and now the purpose of omissions. I will give serious thought as to what I will add. I care not to make omissions of the nature you have made, to do so is to chance throwing away my commission along with yours. Commander Johnson is to sail for Antigua in two days. My report and yours will be in the packet. I've no idea as to what I will write for I shall not lie and I will not omit anything."

"You've heard me out, that is all I ask. Now, if there is nothing else, sir, I will take my leave." Donland said as he stood.

"Very well, I suppose it will do no good to interview your officers as they will tell the same tale."

"Aye, they'd tell the truth and nothing more," Donland said in reply.

Sumerford was waiting outside the residence. "I see you still have your hair and your arse," he said.

"Aye, and my dignity," Donland answered.

"I've a boat waiting to take us across to Kingston, I'm sure Betty will turn your thoughts from boats and admirals."

"Aye," he managed. He'd forgotten her during his time with Pettibone. Again he said, "Aye!"

"See, you have put it all behind you already with just the mention of her name."

Donland said, "I shall send word back to Mister Powell, what is the name of the inn?"

"The Admiral Benbow."

"Then let us be away before the commodore waylays me."

Betty Sumerford came down the curving stairway holding the hem of her white and blue dress in both hands. Donland could not take his eyes from her; she was more beautiful than he remembered.

Once off the stairs, she all but flew to him, throwing her arms around him as his engulfed her. Her lips found his.

Sumerford finally said after more than a minute of watching, "I think that is sufficient."

Donland parted slightly from Betty but did not release her. He stared into her eyes and she stared into his.

"Perhaps the veranda?" Mathias Sumerford suggested.

"Aye," Donland answered and the pair followed Mathias through the lobby and out onto the shaded veranda where he, after a few moments, left them.

Someone pounding on the door awakened Donland. He turned over, discovered that he was not aboard ship. "Captain!" A voice called, it was David.

"Who is it?" Betty asked after sitting upright.

"David," Donland answered and searched for his britches. He realized it was daylight. "I shall be down in a moment!" he shouted.

"Aye," David answered.

He said to Betty, "I will return unless there is something to prevent me from doing so."

She leaned over and kissed him.

David was waiting in the lobby. He rose and came to Donland before Donland descended the last stair. "I would not have come were it not important. One of the Spanish sloops entered the harbor just after dawn. The captain is waiting for you, he said you should come aboard his ship."

"Do you remember his name?" Donland asked.

"Aye, it was Comacho, he commanded our starboard side guns."

"Then let us attend the Lieutenant," Donland said, as he smelled the heady smell of brewing coffee.

Donland came aboard the sloop with full honors due a post captain. He realized that it was the first time he had received such honor. Keeping to naval custom, he doffed his hat to the Spanish flag and to Lieutenant Camacho who then introduced his second in command, Lieutenant Perez.

Donland introduced David.

In broken English, Camacho said, "Come below, si."

When Donland saw that Perez did not follow, he instructed David to wait on deck. He then followed Camacho below, ducking as he did so to miss the deck beams.

A silver service was laid on a small table. A short man with a goatee dressed in the livery of a servant poured wine into two crystal goblets.

"A toast, si?" Comacho asked. And picked up a goblet and handed it to Donland.

"Aye, to His Majesty King Ferdinand!" Donland said.

"King Fredrick!" Comacho said.

Both drank the wine. Comacho then turned to the servant and spoke in Spanish. The servant translated, "Lieutenant Comacho thanks you for your assistance and for honoring him by coming aboard. He is sent by Captain Quadra, who sends a gift of appreciation with his many thanks for your friendship."

The man then turned and picked up a beautiful sword with gold and silver inlays on the hilt. He handed it to Comacho.

Comacho received the sword and said, "A token between us." He held out the sword. Donland immediately knew it was French in origin and no doubt had belonged to the French frigate captain.

Donland accepted the sword and admired it. He said, "You have honored me aboard your ship. Please convey to Captain Quadra my appreciation for his friendship and for his fine gift."

The servant quickly translated what Donland said. Comacho bowed slightly. He then spoke to the servant who turned and produced an envelope.

Comacho handed the envelope across to Donland and smiled. He spoke and the servant began translating.

"Captain Quadra sends this to you. The envelope contains a personal letter and a report of the re-taking of *Galicia*. The captain explains in the report how you aided us in our desperate fight against great odds. He also states in the report that it was his men and not yours that boarded and captured the French vessel."

Donland was mystified. He managed to say "Aye!" and then swiftly said, "Si!"

Camacho added, "letter in English."

Donland nodded and was about to speak when Camacho extended his hand. They shook and Camacho downed the remains of his wine. Donland followed suit.

"We go," Camacho said in English. Then he spoke to the servant in Spanish. The servant translated, "Captain Quadra sent me and told me to sail with all haste that I might arrive before you faced difficulties with your superiors. I trust I have done so and may report to Captain Quadra that all is well with you."

"Aye, you have arrived in time and I thank Captain Quadro for his concern and thoughtfulness."

The servant translated and Camacho smiled. He said, "We go now."

"Aye," Donland agreed.

As the men rowed back to the quay, Donland read Quadro's letter. It indeed was personal, one of giving thanks and an invitation to dine when they next met. Pettibone need not see it.

Pettibone was in his office when Donland reached the residence. Halston was elsewhere and it lay to the clerk to announce Donland's presence.

"I trust you have something to add to the report?" Pettibone asked.

Donland smiled and asked, "You are aware of the Spanish ship in the harbor?"

"Of course, man, I'm not daft!"

Donland did not smile but said, "Captain Quadra sent the sloop. I have Captain Quadra's report. It is in English and gives a full account of his actions and mine. When you read it, you will see that it was the Spanish who captured the French frigate. *Oxford* assisted but Quadra's officers and men accomplished taking her. The re-taking of *Galicia* was likewise done by the Spanish."

Pettibone considered what Donland said. He glanced down at the envelope, Donland saw the temptation in his eyes to remove the report and read. He pursed his lips and met Donland's eyes. "I shall read it and if I have difficulty with any part of it, I will send for you. But, if it is as you have stated, then I shall have no difficulty writing my report. The omissions are perhaps best left as they are. Seems you achieved a victory that shall not be accorded to you."

"Aye," Donland said. He half-smiled and added, "A victory of sorts but such are those that come my way."

Pettibone did not ask what Donland meant but did ask, "Will you be aboard *Oxford* or will you return to The Admiral Benbow?"

Donland laughed and answered, "*Oxford* is a lady but she does not compare to the warmth of my lady's love." He turned to go.

"Unfortunately, there is another matter," Pettibone said and sorted through packets on his desk. "This came for you, it's from the admiralty."

Donland's pulse raced as he received the wax sealed envelope bearing the Admiralty's stamp. Pettibone offered Donland a letter-opener.

Donland stared at the envelope.

"Open it man, I've duties to attend before I leave to dine!"

Donland slipped the letter-opener under the seal. He extracted the document and began to read, the part that jumped out at him was, *your promotion to captain is hereby confirmed!* He stood staring at the words, re-reading them over and over.

"Isaac?" Pettibone asked.

Donland looked up, he wanted to shout and he wanted to cry but he held it in and simply said, "I'm confirmed."

"Congratulations, now that you are, I am instructed by Admiral Sir Hyde Parker to give you this to the captain of *Oxford*. You will find written orders contained."

"Aye," Donland said as he read the writing on the packet, "*Oxford, Captain Donland Commanding.*"

He dropped the letter containing his conformation and stooped to pick it up. There was a second sheet that he had not read. He began to read without standing, It was signed by the queen and thanked him for his bravery and service. She was delighted to grant Lord Angermanland's promise of command and a promotion.

Donland placed the letter and the confirmation back into the envelope. He had his victory.

Printed in Great Britain
by Amazon

82282327R00099